THE LAST TO GO

Printed in Australia
Cover design by Jess Chaplin
Internal design by Steve Williams
First Printing: August 2023

Little Wolf Productions

Paperback ISBN 978-1-7637658-0-1
Ebook ISBN 978-1-7637658-1-8

 A catalogue record for this work is available from the National Library of Australia

THE LAST TO GO

A. D. LYALL

Acknowledgements

*With much thanks to Callum Scott for his
editorial support and guidance, and for believing
in Rus and Charlie from the very start.*

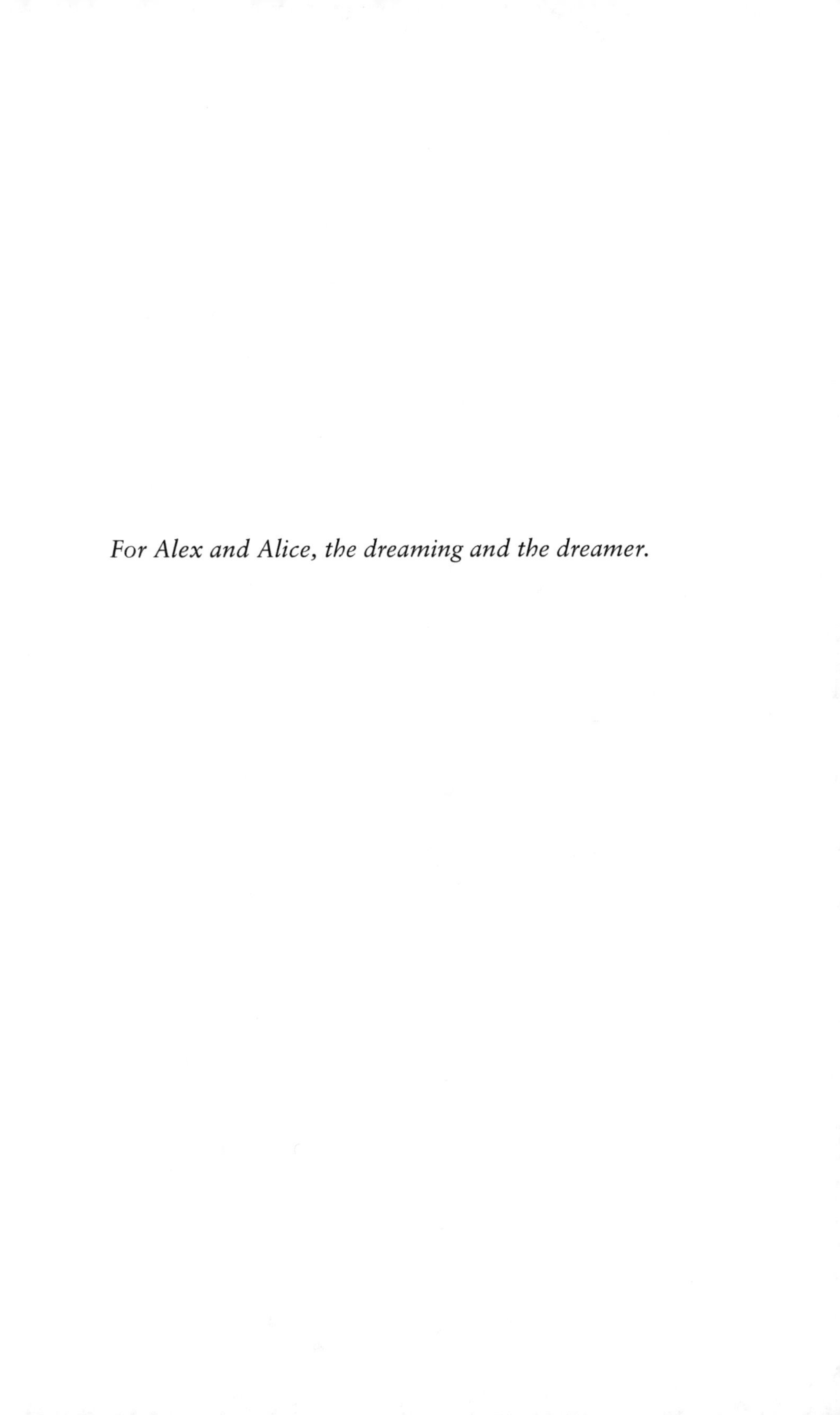

For Alex and Alice, the dreaming and the dreamer.

THE VALLEY I

'I think we need to do a burn-off,' Rus said from the top of the steps. 'I saw a crow this morning.'

Charlie stared up at him, his mouth dropping slightly. 'Are you sure?'

Rus laughed and brushed damp hair from his face. It was early, but the humidity was rising quickly in the golden light of mid-morning. He pointed north of where they stood, to where the sugarcane fields bent closest to the house. 'There's one a few hundred metres from here.'

'Shit,' was all Charlie could say.

Charlie hadn't expected this today, but there was little he could expect any day; going on was enough, so he did what he always did. He'd spent the morning keeping the farm ready in case the world became normal again, maintaining it the way his parents had. He'd checked the perimeter of the property for any obvious intrusions – since it had been subdivided a few years back, this was a simple task. He was glad nothing had been built around the farm before things changed. It still felt like the same place he'd grown up in. But the cane fields were smaller now, contained by dwindling boundaries, like his life with Rus. Life here was measured in sunrises, footsteps, and heartbeats.

Charlie had checked on the horses that lived on the neighbouring property. Their transformation to feral animals was almost complete, and he was relieved by it. The new foal was doing well. He'd tested the water tanks, visited the dam, avoided a snake that arced across a small track, and made sure the gates were shut. Not that the gates or fences could keep anything out. But they mimicked the signs of normalcy, and they would signal a point of intrusion.

The early morning had been normal, the world undisturbed. Charlie had moved through the quiet and made sure all was right with his home. The stillness suited the place, suited him, and he'd felt guilt at that thought. So many people gone. *How can this be a source of happiness for me?*

Now, it was warmer, and much had changed since he'd started his rounds. He hadn't seen signs of entry, hadn't noticed the crow, but part of the northern fence was half down. That must be where it had come through. He ran up the modified steps and into the house. It was instantly cooler inside. Darker, safer. Rus followed him and the wire door snapped shut behind them, locking out insects but little else.

'Did you recognise it?' Charlie asked, heading for the storeroom.

'No. I went to see what Fiddich was barking at – I almost ran into it. I didn't stay to get a better look.' Rus's tone was matter-of-fact, but there was a slight tremble in his hands. 'It may have been Farley. It kind of looked like him.'

Charlie nodded. 'We haven't heard from Ballock Station for a week.'

Rus sighed. 'Their defences were never good.'

'Damn. We always said we'd catch up, but I kept putting it off.' And then, a realisation. 'Did Fiddich go near it?'

'No, I called him back. And *I* didn't either, so we don't need to isolate.'

They entered the storeroom. It was always kept ready for such events. It had been a bedroom once: Charlie's, when he was young, then a guest bedroom. They had renamed it to suit the utilitarian needs of a strange time. Not that many guests had stayed when things were normal. Still, they'd had more than Charlie's parents had when they lived, and when the property had functioned fully as a sugarcane farm.

Charlie often thought back to when he first brought Rus to visit. Rus had got to see into Charlie's existence, away from university and life in a southern city, to experience a working station of the tropics – this was no five-star accommodation. Or even three, or two. And Charlie's parents had got to see who their son was, not just understand it from the perspective of being told. Everyone had struggled during that week of letting others in. Rus, Charlie, his parents. None more than the other, and none exactly as might've been expected. Expectations had been flimsy things even back then. Flimsier now.

The storeroom contained the means to stay alive when expectations failed. Charlie connected a gas cylinder and a hose in the semi-dark. Rus stood in the doorway, his tall frame blocking out the light.

'Sorry,' Rus said, and moved into the room, bringing light with him. He switched the flashlight he was holding from a focussed beam to a cool, radiating glow.

Charlie held Rus's gaze only briefly. His eyes flickered blue, down and away, like oil dropped in water. Slippery. Charlie thought of words of reassurance, went to utter them, but they fell away before they formed.

They continued their ritual of protection. Rus helped Charlie strap one of the gas cylinders to his back: their mini flamethrower, their only reliable weapon. Charlie looked around the shuttered room. There were plenty of cylinders still, but only half as many as a year ago, and they had yet to find more. He couldn't think about that right now. Reality was sometimes best denied, at least when alternatives didn't exist and when hope was in retreat.

When Charlie was sufficiently armed, they left the storeroom and returned to the brightness of the kitchen. Fiddich followed. The German shepherd knew the ritual too; he wagged his tail and whined, his eyes alert. *Trouble is here, or someone is coming. Exciting things might happen. Be ready.*

'I'll take a look, see if I can find other crows,' Charlie said. 'Then we can work out what to do. A partial burn-off or a full one.'

'Hopefully not a full one.'

'Does it matter?'

'The cane fields hide our lights at night.'

Charlie stared down at Fiddich, watching him circle the kitchen. 'Not from the ridge. People can see there's life here.' *Life is still here.*

'It's the wanderers I worry about. They move more along the road; the cane shields us from them.'

'There aren't many of them now, and wanderers can still find plenty of supplies in other houses if that's what they need. They'll leave us alone.'

Rus nodded. 'The virus has done its work.'

Silence fell, broken only by the tapping of Fiddich's claws upon the tile.

'And we've got the rifles and guns. We've got each other,' Charlie ventured at last, wary of what that may provoke.

'We do.' Rus smiled in that elegant way of his and moved to the CB radio sitting on the kitchen bench. 'I like the look of the cane fields,' he said quietly, flipping a switch on the radio. 'They cocoon this house.' A high whistle started to build.

Charlie placed a hand on Rus's shoulder, held it there for

comfort. *Mine or his?* he wondered. He turned towards the wire door.

'Don't disturb it until we know how many there are.' Rus made another adjustment on the radio. 'It's standing just beyond the old bath – you'll see the track I followed. I'll keep Fiddich here and see if I can contact Issy or Grant or Adam. Find out if they know anything.'

The wind had picked up, and the door was rattling slightly, but outside the day remained bright and golden. Charlie walked out of their home – it still felt like that, to him at least – and into the incongruent warmth. He stood briefly on the veranda that encircled the house, made sure the wire door was shut firmly so Fiddich couldn't follow.

Down in the yard, the hens scratched and bathed in dust. The guineafowl, their alert system, gave him wary glances, two of them perched in the Moreton Bay fig. Charlie smiled at the simplicity of this life, its gentle beauty.

He walked down the steps. The sound of the door opening made him turn back. Rus stood there silently, always so elegant and composed despite the life they lived. *He doesn't suit this place*, Charlie thought. More guilt for him to deal with. But sometimes, when the sun hit Rus's copper hair and magnified its colour, when his eyes merged with the sky or the nearby ocean, then the tropical north had full claim on him, made him Arcturus once again. The south drained him.

RUS I
NINE YEARS AGO

They caught up with Rus's sister in Hobart. It was Charlie's first visit to Tasmania, the first time in his life he'd experienced such cold, and even wrapped in a coat and scarf – Rus had insisted on both – the wind bit into him, blowing clear and strong from the Antarctic. They sat by the waterfront, Charlie, Rus and Astrid, unfolding fish and chips from white paper.

'You call him Rus?' Astrid asked Charlie, teasingly.

'Yeah, I do. Icarus, if I'm being serious, but that's all I've known him as.'

She tilted her head at her brother. 'Icca, when did you become Rus?'

'Icca?' Charlie asked. There was always something more to learn about his new partner.

'That's what my family and friends here call me.'

'Mum and Dad would be disappointed that you deny your true identity!'

'Like you can talk.' Rus turned to Charlie. 'Her birth name is Skadi, but she hated it so much growing up our parents agreed to let her use Astrid.'

Astrid laughed. 'I had to keep to the Norse theme, though.' She nudged Charlie. 'You haven't met our parents yet, have you? You'll understand once you do. They're *quirky*.'

'So unusual,' Rus added. 'You should see their house – full of artefacts and books and esoteric crap. They sold up here to buy a bigger place along the north-east coast just so they could store it all.'

'I'd like to meet them. When can I?'

'One family member at a time, Charlie. It's safest that way.' Rus arched a brow at Astrid. 'And our brother, will he be making an appearance?'

'I doubt it. Nathan only appears when he needs something. He's finished his hiking phase and is now into a partying one… or the other way around, it's hard to keep up. Either way, I rarely see him.'

'Nathan? Is that his real name?' Charlie asked, already beginning to understand one of the primal beats of this family.

'Of course not,' Astrid said, with a smile as luxurious as Rus's. 'His name is Nethuns, from the Etruscan god of water, but he shed it a long time ago.'

'The nomenclature of our family – or I suppose you could call it our semiotics – is a complex thing,' Rus explained. 'Sun, winter, water, mythology. Best not to try to make sense of it.'

Astrid, sitting cross-legged but oddly graceful, said: 'But you, Icca, I didn't think you would lose your name.'

'I abbreviated it. I didn't lose it. Easier to fit in, that's all. And it's always been shortened, just at the other end.' Rus chuckled quietly and shook his head. 'Well, I did lose it when I went by Arcturus for a few months.'

Astrid laughed. 'Oh, God, that's right, when you were around ten. Mum and Dad made you keep it Greek! But if I remember correctly, you liked the reference to the star, not the myth…'

'Our parents sure fucked us up, didn't they?'

Astrid looked at her brother for a long time, smiling. She was shorter than him, but just as handsome, and she had similar ways – a warmth of expression, an opulence of manner – and wore the same crown of wavy copper hair.

'Rus is so *common,*' she said, and Rus raised his hand and turned away with a dramatic flourish. The two siblings laughed in the way people always did at an in-joke.

'Common isn't so bad,' he said. 'And even Arcturus had Rus in it.'

Astrid wrapped her arms around her brother and squeezed him tightly.

'Do you have siblings?' she asked Charlie.

'I had an older brother. He died when I was twelve.'

'I'm sorry.'

'It's okay, it's part of life. It just means my parents expect more from me.'

Rus wiped his hands on the crisp white paper, forming greasy windows. 'Don't get me started on parental expectations.' He glanced at his sister, then back to Charlie. In the late winter afternoon, his eyes had changed from the blue of a clear sky to the pallid, shifting grey of a deep forest mist. 'I can't imagine you could get over that, no matter your age.'

The wind rippled the sea below them. There was no warmth in that water. The clouds were light, but the afternoon sun couldn't fully break through. Instead, it shot mournful rays across the harbour and up to Mount Wellington, kunanyi, gilding the snow.

Charlie was happy to be here, to have a glimpse into the lives of such charmingly eccentric people, so different to the ones he'd grown up with. He looked at Rus. Icarus. *This one's a keeper,* his friends had told him, but they hadn't needed to. He knew it to be true. Suddenly, he wanted to learn more about mythology – Greek, Norse, Etruscan – to understand the symbolism that had shaped this man before him. All he knew was that the mythical Icarus had flown too close to the sun. He was sure his Icarus would never do that.

'Do you like what you're studying, Charlie?' Astrid asked.

'The course is okay, but I'm not loving it,' he said. 'Finance seemed like a smart choice, but I'm thinking about changing degrees at the end of the year. Doing something I'm more passionate about.'

'I was a little surprised when Icca chose architecture. Our family always assumed he'd go into the arts. Be an actor, maybe.'

Rus shrugged. 'I like design, and I like order. My course allows me to be creative – just in a different way.'

'And how are you enjoying Sydney?'

'It's great. I like being away from home to study,' Charlie said, and Rus nodded. 'But it's pricey, very pricey.'

Rus pointed at their meal. 'Hence the fish and chips. And the city is much bigger.'

'More tolerant,' Charlie said.

Rus shrugged. 'Easier to disappear into.'

They finished eating and headed back towards Rus and Charlie's hotel. It was extravagant, for two university students, but worth it for Charlie's first visit to this island. His first visit to Rus's home.

Astrid moves like a model, he thought, as the two siblings walked ahead, chatting and laughing. She turned back to Charlie. 'Your family's farm is in Cairns, right?'

'Nah, it's a little further north, in the Mossman valley. You'll have to visit.'

'I'd love to. I've only been as far as the Whitsundays.'

'I'd also love to, but you haven't asked me yet,' Rus said.

'Family intros, Icarus. You know they need careful planning.'

Rus smiled. 'I do, I really do. But I'm glad you got to meet part of mine.'

'The best part,' Astrid added.

'The most normal part,' Rus said. 'The best, or the worst, is yet to come.'

THE VALLEY II

Rus walked out onto the veranda. Charlie grinned up at him, relaxed, confident, a peaked cap pulled over his dark hair, dark eyes shining beneath the brim. Rus had never thought Charlie looked like a farmer. But then again, he hadn't known any farmers until he moved here. He'd learnt early in their relationship that Charlie had the soul of someone who belonged outside. And Charlie had a weathered look – perhaps *too* weathered for someone only soon to turn thirty. Plenty of deep lines on tanned skin. Marks of wisdom, of sun and rain and disregard for the risks of melanoma.

'You need fifty-plus sunblock,' Rus had said, every time Charlie had left the house in the first few months they'd been here.

'What about an Akubra? That'd work, right?' Charlie had taunted back.

Skin cancer was no longer a concern for either of them.

Charlie turned away. He headed towards the old bath, one of the small landmarks by which they navigated the property, to where the crow slept.

Rus felt the warmth of the day and wished he could fold into it. But right now, he was cold. 'Be careful, Charlton,' he called, but Charlie was already too far away to hear him. And he knew

Charlie would be careful. It was the main rule when dealing with crows. That, and *be ready to burn.*

It was still cool inside. They never used the ceiling fans now, as a kindness to the generator, but it was early September and the house could manage without it.

Fiddich stayed at the wire door. He whimpered, restless, wanting to follow Charlie and be among adventure and sun. 'You have to stay here,' Rus said, patting the dog absently.

Fiddich had bitten a crow once. It happened during the day, and the crow had been asleep, but Rus and Charlie had feared it would constitute an attack. It hadn't, not that time, but next time it might. And they didn't know if crows still carried the virus, or if animals could be vectors. Fiddich had been forced to stay in the shed for two weeks after that bite. He'd been off the lead this morning; it was fortunate all he'd done was bark.

Rus worked at the radio. He couldn't raise Adam, but he got Issy.

'I haven't heard anything from James or any of the Farleys for a few days.' Issy's voice crackled over the radio. It sounded flat, but there was emotion there, and the static couldn't hide her accent. 'I really hope you're wrong.'

'Me too. He was a good man.'

'He was a bigot,' Issy said. 'Kate was great, and Sara.'

The radio screeched and the connection dropped out. Rus got it back in time to hear Issy say: 'And if it's not a Farley, it still means someone's lost.'

'It also means the virus is still out there, creating more crows.'

Issy's voice distorted again. 'I thought the crows might be dying out. Grant and I haven't seen any for a month at least.'

'Have you heard from Adam?' Rus asked.

'A few days ago. You don't think it could be him?' Issy's voice was suddenly urgent.

'Wrong body shape and height. Even putrefied, he wouldn't look like what I saw.'

That got a small laugh. 'He had fuel for the Cessna when I last spoke to him. I think he may have taken it to the cape, just to check things out.'

Rus felt such relief at hearing that. *At Adam being alive, or at the plane being operational again?* he wondered, before deciding: *Both.*

'Don't take any risks,' Rus told her. Another unnecessary suggestion, especially for Issy, but he needed to say it. 'Will you and Grant come to dinner when all of this is done?'

'We'd love to. I'll have finished the map by then. We could celebrate like old times.'

The old times were just that, Rus thought. Old. Old enough to be dead and gone. He remembered first meeting Issy at her and Grant's house over the ridge. It happened almost three years ago now, the first time he hadn't felt completely *other* in this place. Like him, Issy had married into a local family. She'd slipped into acceptance much quicker than Rus had; she made people feel at ease. But she wasn't from here, and in that sense, she carried the mark of an outsider just as Rus did.

'Sounds good,' Rus said. 'Charlie will be happy about the map. I'll keep trying, but see if you can get a hold of Adam.'

'We should check in each day. Keep up with whatever's happening.'

'Definitely. At four?'

Issy agreed. Grant called out something, cheeriness in his voice, but Rus couldn't make out the words.

The radio clicked off. The house was quiet. He called Fiddich, but the dog kept vigil at the door.

Rus wanted to join the burning of the crow. He completed a perimeter check of the veranda first; everything seemed sound. The stilts that held their house were strong, and there were no overhangs from trees. They retracted the stairs every night, so Rus knew they were working. He looked out over the western cane fields. Out towards the ridge and its forests. It was peaceful there, and it reminded him of when they'd first come to this place. Back to Charlie's home ground, to honour familial responsibilities, to connect with the land and be together.

Rus hurried through the yard, past the bathtub, full of brown water and wriggling mosquito larvae. Not far ahead, a scream rose. Anguished, inhuman, deeply *wrong*. Fiddich howled from the house in response. Rus shut his eyes and let out a long-held breath.

Thank God. Just one, then.

CHARLIE I
THREE YEARS AGO

Rus unlocked the door to the apartment, entering with speed and little time to prepare, but Charlie was already there, so his plans for a surprise – hasty and last minute, through no fault of his own – collapsed.

'You're home already?' he asked, and handed Charlie the bouquet of flowers he'd picked up on the way home. Peaceful blues for the ocean, a splash of yellow for celebration, and glossy green leaves for the environment. He doubted Charlie would pick up on the symbolism, but it was important to him. The bouquet was large and made the apartment seem smaller.

'Congratulations, Charlie. I'm so proud of you.' Rus hugged Charlie, kissed him, looked into his eyes, and smiled. Charlie's embrace seemed off; a slight tension ran through it. He took the flowers and the champagne. His returning smile was almost abstract, but his eyes were warm.

'It's champagne,' Rus was compelled to tell him. 'Not sparkling wine.'

'Of course it is. I'd expect nothing less from you. Thanks.' Charlie moved to the kitchen area and opened the fridge.

'It's for now – we're celebrating,' Rus said, removing his backpack and jacket.

Charlie gave his deep laugh and took flutes from the overhead cupboards. 'Whisky would've done me just fine.'

'I have that too.' Rus pulled a bottle from his backpack. 'A few glasses of champagne first, then we're going to Fargo for dinner. I booked for seven. We can finish with whisky when we come home.'

'Thanks,' Charlie said again. Rus suspected he'd been on the verge of saying something more, but didn't chase it. They spoke about their days as they drank the champagne, changed for dinner, and headed out into the night.

When they were seated at Fargo and sipping more champagne, Charlie seemed to relax a little. 'It's nice to be here,' he said.

'It is.' A simple reply, full of simple truth.

Outside, it was surprisingly cold for a Sydney winter, but inside was filled with warm light and soothing chatter. The restaurant radiated familiarity. The waiters knew Charlie and Rus, knew them by name, and seated them at their favourite spot. Not right by a window, but close enough for them to glance out and watch the people walking by.

'I'm really proud of you. You know that, don't you, Charlie?'

Charlie shook his head, his usual response to attention and praise. 'I haven't passed yet. Just handed it in, is all.'

Rus took his hands. 'That's an achievement in itself, completing your thesis. You'll pass.'

Charlie rolled his eyes.

'Cheers to having a master's degree under your belt.' Rus raised his glass again.

'It'll just be another piece of paper to hang on the wall.'

'Whatever it is, it marks the culmination of a journey, and your academic one has been… *interesting.*'

'Studying finance wasn't interesting.'

'You did that for your parents. You did environmental science for you.'

Tension rippled over Charlie's face.

'Your dad would've been proud too. I'm sorry, I know that must make this bittersweet.'

Charlie nodded. He sipped his water, and the glass caught the warm light, scattered it across the table.

Rus rarely saw Charlie like this – subdued, even pensive. He wanted to enquire about it, but he'd learnt over many years to let things be. Charlie would reveal his inner world in his own time. Or not at all.

The waiter poured champagne, then wine, and the two got lost in musings and memories. Their conversation went from plans for an overseas holiday to politics to zoonotic transfers to habitat degradation, getting deeper and darker as it went on, then returning to the lighter topic of apartment renovations.

'I think we should redo the kitchen. That island bench takes up too much space,' Rus said. 'The whole place is badly designed. Some changes would make the next year much easier, and then we can sell.'

Again, that tension eddying through Charlie. Rus almost broke his rule and asked about it, but Charlie said: 'From architect to festival planner… that's not a straight-line journey either.'

'I guess not, no.' Rus felt himself start some form of internal preparation. It swam around in his skull, through the alcohol and confusion, but having no target, it remained aimless. *What's coming?*

'Have you locked in those light installations?' Charlie asked.

'This morning, yes. They're going to look amazing. But honestly,

I'll be glad when the festival's over.'

'You wanted a distraction, an artsy one, and you got it.'

'And I've loved having it. But I've already had enough time here. I want to go back south, like we agreed.'

'We will,' Charlie said, unconvincingly. 'In another year.'

'A year's a long time.'

Charlie didn't respond. He just stared at his drink.

'It'll give me time to see out my contract, so that's not a bad thing, I guess. It's just that Sydney doesn't feel like home.'

'Home,' echoed Charlie, staring at his glass.

Here it comes, Rus thought.

It didn't. They left Fargo and stopped for a drink at a bar two blocks from their apartment. It was a popular spot, and had once been Rus and Charlie's favourite. They had gotten drunk there, talked and danced there, laughed together. But its time was over; Rus hadn't known that until this moment. Unlike Fargo, the bar lacked warmth. It was crowded and loud and it moved with an unhealthy pulse.

'This place has lost its soul,' Rus said, firing ambiguity into the air, trying to stir a response, to help him find that target.

'I'm not sure it ever had one,' Charlie replied. 'Maybe we've just outgrown it.'

Rus considered this. He looked around at the people there, attractive, confident, too loud, too obvious. They lacked *layers*. Rus wanted to be away from all of it, knew Charlie did too. But it wasn't just the bar Rus wanted to be away from.

Back in the apartment, Charlie poured whisky. He looked intently at Rus as they sat on the couch together. 'Icarus,' he started, tone already serious. 'You know that virus Mum had?'

Rus nodded. 'Is everything okay?'

The target for his internal preparation was taking shape at last.

'She's getting more tests. She can't seem to shake the fatigue it caused.'

Rus leant forward. 'Why didn't you tell me sooner? I could see something was up.'

'I spoke with her earlier today. She sounded okay, but I'm worried about her. She needs help around the house.'

There it is.

'Of course. We can go there tomorrow – I'll book flights now...' Rus trailed off, sensing there was more.

'I want to stay with her until she sells the place. Would that be okay with you?'

'For how long?' Rus said. He knew he sounded selfish, but he struggled with a moment of resentment. To change his agreement with Charlie now, to change their plans – it seemed unfair.

'They sold the outer parcels of land within a year, so that should be enough time.'

'A year?' was all Rus could say.

Charlie sat there, his mask of strength and stability, along with the many masks that sat under it, suddenly falling away. 'I have to go,' he said. 'She's alone. I can't leave her to this, not with Dad gone.'

Rus stood up and paced the small living area. His world was destabilising, the ground under him breaking and dropping. Their agreement. Charlie's values, his mother in need. A tension between two points, the latter unspoken, but there.

Charlie's eyes were red. 'I'd really like you to come with me. Would you? Please?'

Rus knew that making the request cut Charlie as much as it did him. Charlie was desperate, and that was something new.

'We were planning to move to Hobart,' Rus said, more to himself.

'I know. We still can, in a year or so. We were going to stay here for another year anyway, so it's not too different...'

'It's very different. It depends how quickly you can sell the place. I'd have to leave my job. And it's the far north.'

'You always like it up there when we visit.'

'I do, but it's not where I want to live. It's so far from where I want to live. I can't be myself there.' *I can't hide.*

Charlie stared at his hands. Rus looked at him, saw him more clearly than ever. A farmer was living in this small apartment. A man born of the land, tied to his sense of place and his family in a way that Rus couldn't share. Charlie stayed in this city, studied here, for Rus. There had already been sacrifice.

Rus shut his eyes.

'I'll come,' he said.

THE VALLEY III

Charlie pushed out of the cane field to find Rus heading towards him.

'So, just one?' Rus asked, or stated. It was hard to tell.

'I reckon that's all. I looked around but couldn't find any others.'

'If there were any nearby, you'd have woken them.'

Charlie shrugged. He turned to look at the fields around them, the black ruin he had caused. 'True. But the whole field stinks of decay.'

'It didn't smell like this earlier. That's not a good sign.'

Pulling his cap off, Charlie raked a hand through his hair. 'I think we should go for a full burn-off.' He looked for signs in Rus's eyes, signs of how he was faring, but found none.

'Given the circumstances, I'm okay with that. When?'

'I think there'll be a storm tonight – there are massive clouds building out towards the coast – so there's no point in doing it today.'

'Was it Farley, do you think?'

'Looked like him.' Charlie started to unstrap the gas cylinder from his back. 'It only had a few thorns growing from its hands, so it was newish. But it's hard to tell when they're…'

'No longer human?' Rus said, half-laughing. 'Did it open its eyes?'

'Yeah. When it was burning.'

'I hate when they do that.'

The two briefly watched the black smoke rising from the field.

Charlie raised a hand to cover his nose. 'They're changing again.'

'In what way?'

'I don't know how to explain it. They look more organic, almost like their bodies are woven with plant material. It's more than just having thorns. Maybe they're chimeric.'

'Chimeras in our backyard – my parents would've loved the mythology of it all!' More seriously, Rus added: 'Or maybe the crows are going back to the earth, just like you said.'

The breeze, slowly gaining strength, blew the smoke away, but the scent of charred and decaying matter spilled out from the fields and rolled over them. They walked around the yard, making sure there was nothing lurking. The door of the small shed was closed. They looked inside to be sure and found it clear. The large shed – they never called it a barn – was wide open. Its doors had been removed when Charlie's dad was alive. It was airy and offered few places to hide. The renegade bamboo, a foolish planting that no one could get rid of now it was entrenched, seemed clear, as did the small orchard and the thicket of gums and myrtles.

'I'll go out for a more thorough check later,' Charlie said.

'Let's pull up the drawbridge early this afternoon. I know they don't usually move in the sun, but things feel very wrong out there. Or I feel wrong.'

Charlie smiled. 'Yeah, everything's wrong right now. I'll turn off the generator in case it's drawing them here. We can check the fields tomorrow.'

Fiddich barked and howled from the house, desperate to be with his pack. He quietened only when they reached the top of the steps. Charlie opened the door and he bounded out, tail wagging, ears down. 'It's okay,' Charlie said to him.

Rus started to turn the wrench on one side of the staircase – the drawbridge, as they called it – and Charlie did the same on the other.

'It's not okay,' Rus said. 'Not really.'

Slowly, the stairs started to lift from the ground.

'I know. Give it time. It'll be okay, in time.'

The drawbridge clicked into the fully-raised position. Charlie felt his own tension lift slightly; he hadn't realised it was there. They were safe for now. As safe as they could be.

'I spoke to Issy,' Rus said. 'She and Grant haven't seen anything weird. They're fine.'

He handed Charlie a glass of tank water.

'Did you get through to anyone else?' Charlie asked, an ambiguously framed yet pointed question. Rus saw through the ambiguity, of course.

'I couldn't raise Adam, and Issy hasn't seen him for a few days.'

Charlie always reacted to that name. Undetectably, he hoped. 'He's probably out hunting or something.'

'A bad time to be in the bush. Issy thinks he might've taken the Cessna out.'

'It can fly again?'

'He found more fuel, apparently.'

Charlie dragged out a stool and sat at the kitchen bench.

He drank his water in silence.

'It's a good thing,' Rus added. 'We can explore more, go on another mission.'

'Next time it's my turn.'

Rus nodded. The windows rattled lightly as a gust of wind blew over the house.

Evening came earlier than usual, heavy clouds darkening the world. Charlie and Rus shone flashlights out into the yard, but there was nothing there that didn't belong. Rus had been aloof for most of the afternoon.

'Apart from the obvious, what's wrong?' Charlie finally asked him, trying to conceal his growing annoyance. The day had been hard enough, and the night promised to be more so, even without Rus's sullenness.

'Nothing,' Rus answered. 'I'm just not ready for this again.'

'I know, I really do. I'm not either.' Charlie reached out for Rus, but he turned away.

'The hens have been laying,' he said, over his shoulder. 'I'll make omelettes for dinner, and open that whisky Adam gave us.'

'Gave *me*. The whole crate, or just a bottle?'

'A bottle to start with, but it depends on the night.'

They kept the house dark, except for a few lamps, as they drank whisky and ate. The omelettes were good, and there were no signs of crows.

'Remember when I broke one of these?' Rus said, holding a heavy crystal tumbler with whisky inside, amber like the morning had been.

'Mum was pretty good about it,' Charlie answered, smiling, 'but I think it convinced her she was right to keep her best things hidden at all times.'

'Like tea towels and good cutlery. My mum was the same.' Rus swirled his drink, mouth curving.

'Your mum didn't have tea towels,' Charlie said lightly. 'She had fabrics from far-away places. And a dishwasher.'

'That's true. But I felt terrible about the tumbler. They were your grandma's, right?'

'Yep. Mum still had three, so she was fine. And now they're ours.'

'It's strange, sometimes. Living within other people's pasts, with all their things.' Rus swept his hand around the dim living room, the crystal tumbler held loosely in it, the same graceful flourish that had once ended with a broken glass. 'I wish we could've brought more of ours from Sydney. Shaped it more to us.'

Charlie frowned. 'You hated our place there. And our stuff.' He watched as Rus seemed to seep back into himself, his eyes, despite the darkness, shining again.

'I didn't hate it,' Rus said, lounging further back in the recliner. He flicked the side lever and raised the footrest. 'I just didn't want to stay there.'

'And instead, I brought you north.'

Rus had become Rus again. A little of Arcturus – that bright star – had returned to his smile. 'Your mum needed you. And this place needed someone to keep its soul alive when she was gone.'

'Selling it was harder than I thought.' Charlie meant it had been hard to find someone to buy it, but he might as easily have meant letting it go. The moment was fragile, and he was careful. 'Thank you for doing that. For keeping its soul alive.'

Rus held up his glass, and the two gave a cheers from afar.

'I hope Adam didn't go back to Cairns,' Charlie said.

Rus sat up, tense again. 'He wouldn't, not into the actual city.' Another of the rules: avoid the places where many people once lived.

'But we still don't have answers, even after you flew all over the place with him. The two of you never came up with any theories. That'd eat at someone like Adam. He'd want to know – why are cities so dangerous?'

'It's eating at me too, but we know half of it. It's because there are so many crows there. It's *why* they're there that needs solving.'

The two sat quietly for a long time, sipping their drinks and turning inwards.

By twelve, the night was windy, but the crows hadn't come. Rus headed to bed and Charlie and Fiddich went out to the veranda. Charlie sat on a plastic chair and looked out through the dark at the usual silhouettes. Wind rippled over the cane fields, bringing the sound of frogs and crickets, and the vague smell of earth and rotting meat.

Later, the guineafowl, roosting in the nearby trees, raised the alarm and woke Charlie. It was around 3.30 a.m. Rain was pelting the tin roof, accompanied by flashes of brilliance and rolling thunder, and there were noises beneath the house. Rus was deep in dreams. Bad dreams, it seemed, by his thrashing about. He found his way out of them sluggishly, but he got there. They listened for half an hour, lying in bed, not talking, hearing shuffling and dragging, the occasional clanging of metal.

'Testing our defences,' Rus whispered.

'Nah, they're not that bright. They're probably just bumping into things.'

'Seems like we *do* need that full burn-off.'

Charlie laughed quietly.

Fiddich shuddered on the bed between them. Thunder had an effect on him that crows didn't. The storm brought white noise, and sharp noise, to block out the sounds of the things that lurked below. *Small mercies*, thought Charlie, but sleep would not come.

RUS II
TWO AND A HALF YEARS AGO

They arrived early at the hospital in Cairns to bring Charlie's mother home. The virus had left her system, but her body was shutting down, little by little, for reasons that no one could explain. Soon she would be gone.

'Thank you,' she said to Rus, who steered her wheelchair out to the waiting car. 'I know this can't be easy for you.'

'Please don't thank me, Mary. It's my pleasure. I'll do whatever I can to help you.'

Mary Baxter nodded, her skin yellow, her face sunken, but her voice held strength. 'I know you will, and for my son. We're both grateful.'

Charlie was determined to drive. He and Rus lifted his mother carefully into the car, strapped her seatbelt on and folded the wheelchair into the boot. Charlie spoke to her about the farm, about normal things. She nodded but said little, mostly peering out at the landscape they moved through. *It's the last time she'll take this drive*, Rus thought, and looked at the ocean, the winding road, the canopy of trees, the beaches, trying to see it all the way Mary might.

Charlie chattered almost nonstop. Rus wanted him to be quiet and let his mother farewell the beauty, but would never say that. This was *their* journey, in every way. Rus was only a traveller accompanying them, brought in at the last moment and forever playing catch-up. But he could sense Mary saying goodbye to the place. Could read her wistful expression, her distraction. The experience was oddly profound.

They set Mary up in her bedroom. They would provide hospice care, not palliative, and the distinction was important to her. Like her son, she was pragmatic about all things, other than perhaps her shoes – they always made her look elegant and didn't belong in the fields. Rus and Charlie unpacked the hospice kit. Atropine, lorazepam, morphine and more.

Mary wanted to sit out on the veranda in the late afternoon. They made her as comfortable as possible. She seemed peaceful; happy, even. She reclined in a bed of cushions with a light sheet covering her legs. Rus told her she looked like a movie star, with her red lipstick, and her grey hair pulled back.

Charlie brought her a cup of tea, but she sipped at it once and said she'd had enough. 'Just sit with me for a while,' she told him. 'And you too, Rus.'

When they obeyed, Mary said to Charlie: 'I'm glad your father went before me. He wouldn't have coped, being alone.'

'You're right, Mum.'

'He really loved this place. I did too. Still do.'

'Me too,' Charlie said, with an awkward glance at Rus, but it wasn't an admission that surprised him.

'You need to sell when I go. Promise me you will, Charlie.'

'We'll deal with that when it's time.'

'Deal with it now. You moved back here to help me sell it, but nothing's happened.'

'You've been our focus since we got here,' Charlie said gently.

'I know, and I said to Rus earlier that I'm grateful.' She patted Charlie's hand, then reached out for Rus's and did the same. 'But this place isn't right for him.'

'Mary—'

'The area isn't,' she said, cutting off Rus's protest and squeezing his fingers. 'I've seen how people respond to you, and how they've responded to Charlie over the years. I know Charlie's dad sometimes said the wrong thing.'

'Dad's grandfather had it harder here,' Charlie said quietly.

'And *your* grandfather had it hard,' Mary said, 'torn between two worlds.'

'While Dad kept to one. And was torn by that.'

Years ago, the three of them had had a conversation about Charlie's great-grandfather, a Samoan living in Australia during the time of the White Australia Policy, constantly at risk of being deported.

'He claimed to be Māori,' Mary had explained, 'in an attempt to get around that hateful policy. New Zealand citizens could live here. But for him, there was always fear. And a cruel hangover from the dubious days of the early cane cutters.'

'Dad could blend in, but it gave him insights,' Charlie had said.

And Rus had said: 'Blending in isn't the same as belonging. And trying to can be harmful.'

Mary had understood Rus's perspective then. She understood his reality now.

'Sell the place. Leave it. Be happy, please. I was happy for so long, and I want the same for you both.' Mary rubbed her hands together, as if she were cold. 'It's like that poem by Larkin,' she said, not for the first time this week. 'Home is *shaped to the comfort of the last to go*... this place isn't shaped for either of you.'

The evening arrived, and Mary said she was ready for bed. 'In case I don't wake up tomorrow—'

'Mum!'

'In case I don't wake up, one more thing. Get yourself a dog and take it with you when you leave. Take something living with you from the north.'

Mary didn't die that night. They looked after her for a week before she passed. Rus appreciated the chance to get to know Charlie's mother; it gave rich insights into his man. And he enjoyed Mary's time, as short as it was. Whereas Rus's mother was scattered and intense, Charlie's was calm and sensible. He wished he'd had more time with her.

When Mary did go, it was on a Thursday morning, a 'yellow' day for a semi-synesthete like Rus. Peaceful, because of the colour. Rus rang his parents and told them he missed them and wanted to see them. They sounded vulnerable on the phone, unsettled by the increasing rates of infection. Another strange virus was loose across the country. They wanted their son with them, just as Mary had wanted hers.

'I'll come as soon as I can,' Rus promised them. 'We both will.'

THE VALLEY IV

In the morning, Rus lowered the bridge, and Charlie, armed with fire once more, explored under and around the house. The rain had stopped hours ago, but the clouds remained dark and low. They skimmed over the ridge and promised to break open again.

There were numerous sets of footprints in the muddy yard, some made by boots or shoes, some by bare feet, or perhaps a mix of both. The prints marked the retreat of the night visitors, pointing towards the cane fields.

Charlie sighed. 'Way too wet for a burn-off. We'll have to wait at least a few days.'

Rus rubbed his eyes with the palms of his hands, wiping away tiredness and night images that flickered in his mind. 'We still don't know how many there are. We can do that today – start to count them.'

'Sounds good. An unplanned burn-off can be risky.'

'So is leaving crows in your yard.'

'We'll get rid of them soon enough. At least the rain will dampen the smell,' Charlie said. He did what he always did. He went on, planned for the day and made things work as they should.

Something was building within Rus, though. Each day, it rose a little closer to the surface. He'd tried to ignore it, but it was there, unformed, its shape almost visible. *What shape? What is it?* He'd lived with a sense of detachment for some time now, knew that Charlie did too, and wondered if something was breaking through, or his defences were breaking down. Or both.

And Rus knew that he and Charlie were faced with more than a changing world. They were deep into a new way of being; each was reimagining his man.

'I'll take the back fields,' Charlie said. 'You okay to take the front?'

'Sure. I'll check over the road too. Breakfast first?' It was a token, not to broker peace – there was no fight, no harshness, no need for mending – but it suddenly seemed important.

'Eggs, right?' Charlie flashed a smile, bright, warm and simple.

'Eggs indeed. Scrambled or fried?' Rus already knew the answer, but he feigned surprise, raised an eyebrow when it came.

'Fried.'

Charlie headed towards the outdoor shower, a tank with a makeshift nozzle protruding from one side. Rus went to collect eggs. He walked past the broken ute, the broken horse trough, so many broken things, and on towards the chicken coop. The hens were already out; the door had long since fallen off, another thing to be repaired one day. There were plenty of eggs. In contrast to the coop, none of them were broken.

He stared out into the western field. No sign of crows. But there was a magpie, making angry noises, swooping down to clip its beak over the cane before gliding arrow-like back to the Moreton Bay fig. The guineafowl protested its arrival but soon settled into their usual ways. The flock had over fifteen birds now, and Rus liked them more than he did the domestic fowl, or the chooks, as Charlie called them.

'They're monogamous,' Rus told Charlie over breakfast.

Charlie looked up from his eggs, eyes blank, or inwardly

focussed, but not annoyed, never annoyed by Rus's occasional odd and arcane revelations.

'Guineafowl,' Rus filled in for him.

'Not the crows, then?'

'Maybe them too.'

'Is that why you call them *Charlie birds?*'

'I call them that because they stay close to home. But they have strong wings, not like the chickens – I mean, the chooks. The guineafowl could fly away if they wanted.'

'Ah.'

'They can be polyandrous, though. The guineafowl. Ours are, I think; the females have a number of males in their retinue.'

Charlie shot Rus a look of affection, warm and quick, like he used to show often, years ago, when the world was young and still forming. Lightness flickered between them.

'You know some bizarre shit,' Charlie said.

'It's our knowledge and how we use it that set us apart from other species, Charlton.' Rus projected mock indignity.

'Then humanity is truly doomed, with me in the survivor pool.'

Now it was Rus's turn to behold Charlie with affection. Of all the masks he wore, and he had several, this was the strangest: his pretence at stupidity, combined with his determination to fit into the northern landscape. It was especially apparent in the way he spoke. Charlie was accomplished at code switching. He matched the vernacular of his surroundings when he chose to, a chameleon of sorts. Since returning to the north, he'd made an enduring switch. To reconnect with the place, Rus assumed. It was another façade, but Rus wouldn't question it – he had many of his own. Sometimes, though, Charlie would slip, switching to a different code, when he was with Issy or at his most serious. Then science and art and insight would pour out from him.

'I think you represent our species well enough,' Rus said, and Charlie smiled.

The two finished their meal and walked out the back door. Charlie started making his way towards the western fields. Fiddich followed Rus as he turned towards the driveway.

'We'll head out to the road,' Rus called. 'See you in twenty.'

The rain was coming back. Slow, heavy drops, at first, but the clouds were dark and full, and soon they would cause rivulets to run again. The humidity was back again, too. Heavy. Close. Rus's raingear was a shield against the weather that weighed him down, stifled him. He pulled it off and dropped it as he started down the long driveway. He wanted to feel the rain when it resumed fully.

Rus checked the cane fields that ran along one side of the driveway. He looked for disturbances, broken cane, anything that might mark the presence of a crow. He looked to Fiddich for warning signs. There were none.

Three guineafowl scurried ahead of Rus and Fiddich, making noises of concern and indignation. They took to the wing, flapping heavily over the cane field, arced back around and flew towards the house.

'Fly home, Charlie birds,' Rus called after them.

He carried a long branch, which he pushed gently into the greenery at random points. There was an art to this searching. The survivors of the valley – of the ridge, the cape and the tablelands – had discovered this art through harsh lessons. Crows *could* be woken during the day. If Rus felt resistance, he knew to withdraw slowly. He checked the scattered vegetation opposite the field. There was nothing there.

At the entrance to the property, where the driveway hit the road, Rus stopped. Passing through the entrance was suddenly difficult. He felt exposed, vulnerable. He carried a revolver, which offered some sense of security, but not much. The property opposite was overgrown; not with cane, but with pastures and weeds. The cows there hadn't managed to change into wild things. They had died out six months ago, lying bloated and rotting in the fields. Now they were bleached bones framed with stretched leather.

The clouds dropped lower, gathered more greyness, and the mid-afternoon light fled. Rain started to fall with a heavy and constant drumming. Rus and Fiddich walked the straight section of road in front of the property, taking quick steps. They were both drenched, and the searching was made difficult by the storm's slow return. Rus wanted to be off this road, to be obscured again by cane. He had done all he could. There were no crows to be found.

The sound of a light aircraft came suddenly over the field of cow carcasses. Rus searched the horizon, but there was little chance of seeing anything through the low clouds.

'Adam,' he said aloud, and Fiddich looked up at him.

The plane was returning, getting closer to the ground, a steady approach for landing. Not in Mossman, somewhere much closer. Rus wouldn't have time to get back to the house and call Adam, to warn him or to just to speak to him. Hopefully, Issy had let him know what had been happening. Thunder sounded, scattering Rus's thoughts.

It became darker still; a false twilight covered the land. Rus led Fiddich quickly back to the driveway. He caught movement within the cane. At first, he thought it was a bird, small and dark, but he soon realised it was a hand protruding from the fluttering stalks. Fiddich barked at the vague shape. It pushed out of the dull wet green, slowly. The world rumbled again and Rus ran, calling Fiddich. The two of them ran in thunder, ran back towards the house, wind and rain and darkness surrounding them.

ADAM I
TWO YEARS AGO

The Exchange Hotel was half full. Charlie noted Mossman locals mostly, perhaps a few tourists, along with the five of them sitting out in the beer garden. Thankfully, the humidity was dropping with the sun. Issy and Grant had brought their friend, Adam Keeslar, to introduce to Charlie and Rus.

'He moved here from Melbourne a year ago, and he's smart,' Issy had explained at a barbeque only a few weeks earlier. By that she meant they might form a connection. Rus might, especially. A bond of outsiders, which could help his transition into living here. She'd also explained, in that musical accent of hers, that Adam had been a helicopter pilot in the army, but it was a sensitive topic that shouldn't be asked about. She'd assured them that his current job, flying light aircraft for tourists, was safe ground.

Charlie was struck first by Adam's height. He was even taller than Rus, and that was a rare thing to see. Like Rus, he was intelligent, witty and quick to smile. But there was something guarded about him, something hidden and distant, an occasional hardness of tone. And his handshake, when it came, was overly forceful. He was older than them by around ten years, Charlie guessed. With his black hair and green eyes, and the strange grace with which he moved, he reminded Charlie of a panther.

Issy was skilled at introductions, and skilled at managing conversations. She deftly manoeuvred their small talk to reveal insights that might help form bonds, but kept it well away from Adam's army background. Adam made no reference to it at all.

A schooner of beer in hand, Adam motioned towards Issy. 'A Swedish friend once told me that no one could ever be mad at a Norwegian, thanks to their accents.'

Issy tilted her head. 'I wonder if having a Korean mother means it only half works for me? What do you think, Grant?'

Grant raised both hands in a placating gesture. 'Fully. For sure.'

'Right answer,' Adam said.

Adam was charming. And now he charmed the two charmers. Rus and Issy both laughed at his anecdotes and gentle jibes, and the evening took on a familiar air, but only between those three. Grant and Charlie were outside of the bonding, and it felt like Adam wanted it that way. It stirred something in Charlie. Not jealousy. That wasn't his way, it never had been. But he was reacting to *something*. He couldn't define it, and although it was small, he wished he could make it out.

And so, he changed tack: *Get to know this man, get to understand what drives him.*

'How long do you plan to stay up here, Adam?'

'I'm not sure, to be honest. I love the place, and some of the people are *okay*.' Adam gave a wry smile, nodded towards Issy. 'Like Issy, and hopefully you guys.' He winked. 'But I can't get used to the temperature.'

'Tell me about it,' Rus chimed in. 'It's the humidity that kills me.' In a quieter voice, he added: 'And the judgment is more obvious...'

Adam seemed to miss Rus's last comment. 'But I like my work,' he said. 'I like flying, and I get to see some amazing landscapes.

For now, I'll take my time.'

Issy placed a hand on Adam's forearm. His whole right arm was covered in intricate tattoos, entwined creatures overlaid with numbers and other indistinct things. There was a white cross, buried under newer designs. 'I don't want you to go,' she said. 'Outsiders like us bring in new ideas, new things to talk about. Don't we, Rus?'

Rus nodded and sipped his beer. 'We bring culture to the place.'

The three outsiders laughed, and it annoyed Charlie.

'There's culture here,' Charlie said, hearing his voice become sharp. 'And history that stretches tens of thousands of years.'

Rus picked up on it. 'There is, you're right. Ours is a very limited perspective. The Kuku Yalanji people have culture in spades. I'm sorry.'

Charlie relaxed. Rus was reading him and reattuning his charm.

Adam nodded. 'They gave us Cathy Freeman and Jessica Mauboy, among others.'

So, the ex-soldier knew something about the place. As a tour guide, he should, but it was obvious stuff. Was there anything more? Anything substantial?

If there was, Adam didn't mention it. He started to speak about the rainforests, the river, the gorge, talking like a guide, telling them things that Charlie and Grant already knew, that Rus and Issy probably did too. Issy steered the conversation into safer waters, and they started to talk about music. Adam and Charlie shared similar tastes. Charlie was annoyed by that.

But there was more. There was something familiar about this man. Issy's warning about taboo topics prompted it: Charlie thought he'd read something about an ex-soldier fleeing from Melbourne, about compromised acts of valour, unproven, but enough to make people talk. Could this be the same man?

Charlie asked: 'What made you come here, Adam? Why'd you leave Melbourne?'

Adam laughed. 'Everyone from the south comes to the north eventually, mate, at least for a while. Don't they?'

The answer was as evasive as Charlie had expected.

'Is that right?' Charlie asked.

'Yeah, mate, of course. It's about the sun and the beach, the slower pace, you know. The usual reasons. But I'm not sure it ever makes us southerners want to stay. Not for long.'

Charlie darted a glance at Rus, tried to read him, but Rus had raised his inscrutable visage.

'Maybe it just doesn't for me.' Adam smiled. 'Or maybe it will. But I can think of other places I'd rather be.'

The evening wore on, cicadas sang, and the air became cool and fragrant. Grant was keen to talk property maintenance with Charlie, station owner to station owner. Issy flitted between two very different conversations, and Charlie tried to attend the second, but missed most of it.

'It would take two full tanks to fly from here to Sydney,' Charlie heard Adam tell Issy and Rus.

And later: 'Melbourne, possibly, but on the coast would be good, or maybe the high country...'

And later still: 'Icarus, like the Greek myth? Your parents were gutsy!'

Adam's voice was louder than Rus's, so Charlie missed much of the in-between conversation. He thought he heard something about Daedalus, but wasn't sure.

Eventually, Adam turned his charm, or his attention at least, back towards Charlie. 'Rusty here was telling me you've got a good collection of vinyls?'

Charlie sensed Adam might invite himself over. 'Yeah, I do.

We do.'

'I'll have to come over and listen to them. I sold all mine when I left Melbourne. I've been hanging out for the scratchy sound of a good record.'

'We can make a night of it,' Charlie said. It was the last thing he wanted, but Adam was hard to deny, especially in the presence of others. Influence, suggestion, deflection. Adam seemed to know so much about these things.

Rus mentioned Charlie's master's degree. He spoke about it with pride, and Charlie downplayed it.

'With everything that's happening in the world,' Adam said, with a casual seriousness, 'it'll probably come in handier than you'd expect.'

Charlie shrugged. 'It doesn't help me fix local environmental issues, so I don't reckon it'll help with global ones.'

'Better than having a pilot license and being dependent on tourists.'

'This whole area takes a hit every time the borders close down.' Charlie saw another in, another way to pry. 'Will you go back before that happens? It could be any week now.'

'I reckon I'll ride it out. There are other things I can do here to make myself useful – I can't let my skills go to waste.'

The evening ended with Charlie and Rus promising to hold a dinner in a few weeks, where Adam could go through their vinyl collection.

'Loud music, wine and beer,' Issy commanded of the promised night, and Rus agreed.

The group stood. Two tall men, two disarming men, shook hands and embraced.

'Keep away from the sun, Rusty,' Adam called over his shoulder. 'The south remembers.'

As he vanished into the darkness, a new image of Adam formed in Charlie's mind. He resembled a python with his sleekness, with the way his jade eyes captured people.

Rus sidled up to Charlie, took his arm, and smiled into the night, already hypnotised.

THE VALLEY V

The storm was overhead when Charlie headed down the driveway, finished with his initial search. He'd spotted three sleeping crows, but suspected there were others deeper within the fields, and had heard a plane that sounded like it was about to land. That realisation had surfaced feelings of relief and suspicion. Charlie was concerned by the latter.

The day had become oddly dark. Above, the sky was grey, on the horizon it was orange, and in the middle, there was rain and wind and wavering lightning. The guineafowl had been fooled by the diminishing light and headed to the trees to roost. Other creatures might be fooled into believing night was here too.

Rus and Fiddich came into view, running up the driveway with a strange grace – Rus on long legs, Fiddich almost greyhound-like. They were both soaked but carried an energy that felt like the storm's.

'I heard the engine,' Charlie began, before they reached him. 'It sounded like—'

'The crows are moving.'

Charlie scanned the area quickly, then ushered Rus back towards the house. 'They won't be fully awake yet. They never are until it's completely dark. How many did you see?'

'Just one. You?' Rus's voice was clear despite his running, but his chest heaved. Fiddich panted.

'I saw three. There's nothing more we can do today. Let's pull up the bridge.'

When the stairs were raised and they'd patted Fiddich down with a towel, when they'd both changed into dry clothes, they sat once again at the kitchen bench. It was a little lighter outside. The storm had lost some of its fury, but the rain was constant, and the lightning and thunder continued.

'We have an infestation, then,' Rus said, as he tried the radio.

'Seems like it. We'll deal with it as soon as we can. We have plenty of supplies.' Charlie hesitated, then said: 'He landed close by.'

'I wished he'd stayed with his plane. I can't get on to him.'

'Nothing from Issy?'

'No. She isn't due to call in for another hour.'

'I could take the truck, see if I can find him – there's only a few places he could've landed in the area.'

Rus looked brighter at the suggestion. 'That might be a good idea.'

'I assume he's trying to get to our place… or maybe to the Aldis farm.'

Rus's eyes slipped away and back to the radio.

'He'll be fine,' Charlie added, because he knew Rus needed the reassurance. He believed his own words, or wanted to.

It always felt strange to say Adam's name, so he avoided using it. As did Rus, but for different reasons. Charlie counted Adam an acquaintance. He was just someone who existed within the background noise of life. Handsome, a pilot, always on the move, flirtatious, smart, and connected. Adam and Rus, *connected*. There was nothing there, Charlie told himself. But Rus flirted too.

And he couldn't shake *that* conversation. He'd heard it, the night of playing vinyl records. Snatches of it. The plans, possible plans, of other places and escape. Or he'd made the conversation into all that, had remembered it in a way that made it significant. Had given it meaning and threat, when perhaps it'd been benign. It had happened after many drinks of wine and whisky in this very house, and had involved neither code nor cipher. Just the words of drunk people who thought they were protected by loud music. Nevertheless, its meaning, if there was any, was obscured. The words had been like hieroglyphs, symbols that didn't make sense without the Rosetta Stone to interpret them. Charlie still looked for that stone.

He headed out into the afternoon rain to search for Adam, with Fiddich by his side. Petrol was scarce, but this was important to Rus, and to Charlie, for different reasons. So he took the truck and searched. He couldn't see the crow at the end of the driveway, but with the clouds lifting slightly, it was probably sleeping again until true night fell. The windscreen wipers pushed away the rain and the headlights cut away the gloom, but that feeling – doubt? betrayal? – remained firm.

Life still went on beyond the farm, but it was only the life of plants and insects and animals, unless you knew where to look. Charlie sounded the horn each time he drew close to somewhere he thought the plane could land. There was no sign of the plane or its pilot, and Charlie didn't drive as far as the Aldis farm. They were strange people, the Aldis family; had been strange people before the world darkened and were even more so now.

'I couldn't find him,' Charlie said to Rus when he returned. 'Did you have any luck?'

Rus raised blue eyes from the CB radio, deeply blue and briefly sad. 'No,' he replied simply. 'No word from Issy either. And it's past four.'

'You're expecting too much,' Charlie said, and regretted it. 'I mean... she's probably busy, working the farm or something.'

More gently, he added: 'And Adam knows what he's doing – he's a survivor.' He said his name and lived through it.

Charlie was taken by the urge to ask questions, to find that Rosetta Stone and gain understanding. Instead, he poured whisky: Adam's gift, and an enduring irony within this house. The whisky was good, *uisge beatha*, in the old tongue. It brought calmness of thought and action. Outside, the storm ran itself out, and the real night came down at last.

ISSY 1
SEVENTEEN MONTHS AGO

Charlie and Issy sat on a fallen log, looking out across the 'little valley', as Issy called it. The vista stretched out and upwards. Down the small incline, and over to other smaller spines that ran through the ranges. A lot of the nearby land had been cleared. Cows and horses roamed across the beauty. A mirage of bucolic life existed here but was replaced by the rising wild a few hills away. Magpies warbled and a light breeze moved the treetops, adding to the tranquil song of the land.

Behind Charlie and Issy there was tension, building from the conversations about the strange happenings of the world. It curled out from the group gathered around the barbeque, snaked its way down to them.

'Interesting times,' Charlie said. 'The season is changing.'

Issy, correctly, did not take him literally. 'It's been changing for a while now.'

Charlie peeled back a strip of bark on the log. Little insects, suddenly exposed, scurried for cover. 'We always seem so far away from it all up here.'

'Which means when we *do* feel it, whatever it is, it's because it's significant. Or it's getting close.'

Charlie looked back at the others. Grant flipped steaks and burgers on the grill. Rus stood with James and Kate Farley, doing his best to keep Fiddich from jumping up on them. The dog's youthful exuberance was considerable. Adam spoke to Audrey Aldis. More 'neighbours' arrived, most people Charlie didn't recognise.

'I should be a better host,' Issy said. 'Make sure everyone knows each other.'

'Grant's doing a fine job, Issy. Have a break from it. You always play that role so well.'

Issy smiled. 'I usually love having visitors. But today feels a bit… heavy.'

Rus came and joined them, Fiddich bounding along, a dried pig's ear in his jaws.

'How's the mood?' Issy asked.

'Speculative,' Rus said, with a grin. 'It's okay. The food and drink are keeping spirits buoyant enough.'

'I'm glad you guys could come. I love spending time with you both, and we don't get to do that a lot these days.'

'Same for us,' Charlie replied.

Rus gave an emphatic nod. 'And it's good to do normal things still.'

'We've been through border lockdowns before.' Charlie aimed to be reassuring, hoped he pitched his voice right. 'We've been through heaps of outbreaks, and the viruses always die off, or we make vaccines. This will be the same.'

Rus sat close to Charlie and breathed in deeply. 'It's weird that something carried in the air, something we can't see, gets into us and does so much damage.'

'It's weird that we don't know *what* it does to us,' Issy added.

'Each time, the effect is new.'

'What do you think it will be this time?' Rus asked. 'Cataracts? A reduced capacity to see the light spectrum, or an increased one? We might be able to see UV rays.' He was trying so hard to be positive.

Issy put a hand on his shoulder. 'You were going to visit your family soon, right? I'm sorry that won't happen.'

Charlie watched for Rus's response.

'Thanks. Yeah, I was. Maybe in a few months I can.'

'And what about you, Issy?' Charlie asked. 'You're even further from home. When did you last see your family?'

'Almost three years ago. I think I need to visit again, as soon as I can. But the Norse countries seem to be doing okay. Sweden has changed tack, and Norway is as safe as any place can be right now.' Issy ruffled Fiddich's ears. 'I should brush up on my Korean, though. It's been so long since I visited any relatives on my mum's side. Still, Norway's home.'

'You've managed the tropics well, for someone from such a cold place,' Charlie said, and wished he hadn't. Rus might think the comment was aimed at him, an observation of contrasts.

'This is all an adventure for me.' Issy laughed. 'Even my marriage is an experiment, a new experience. I might change my mind, or life might change my situation, at any moment. That's all we can live by – the moment.'

Issy's comment, her perspective, felt hollow to Charlie. But he understood it. She wasn't being flippant; she was living in the *now*. Being pragmatic, the thing Charlie should be. They had once spoken about existential theory. It appealed to them both, parts of it. Rus understood the theory but rejected it. He saw meaning in life.

At that moment, Adam walked over. 'I'm not interrupting anything, am I?' he said, with that deep voice of his.

Charlie wanted to say *yes* and *go away*, but he remained civil. Besides, it was too late: Adam hadn't waited for an answer. He took a seat on the log next to Rus.

'Nah, not at all,' Charlie said, unconvincingly.

Issy filled Adam in on the conversation. Adam said something in a language that Charlie couldn't understand, but took to be Norwegian.

Issy laughed. 'That was Danish. You know I'm from further north, right? But yes, I'd love another drink.'

Adam returned carrying four beers, and Issy took one with a wide smile. '*Tusen takk*,' she said. Charlie recognised that, at least. Issy had taught him *thousand thanks*.

The conversation moved and veered in a pleasant way, despite Adam's presence. Issy laughed more with Adam. He made the mood lighter; he had a skill in that way, at least with some people. Rus laughed too, an opulent laugh.

He makes love to them both with his words, Charlie thought, but noted that Grant never seemed to react. He wasn't sure whether Grant held it in or if he was alone in these transient insecurities.

Family came up. Adam was silent about his, but asked questions of Rus and Issy. Expectations rolled around. Issy had fled some of those, like the expectation to have children.

'Being far away helps me avoid the disappointment in their eyes,' she said. 'FaceTime and Zoom don't make it as obvious.'

Rus laughed at that and said both he and Charlie hoped to avoid the outcomes of their namesakes. Charlie really didn't want to get into that, but Issy leapt on it.

'I know yours of course, *Icarus*, and apparently, coming up north brings you even closer to your fate. But Charlie, what's your namesake?'

Charlie shook his head. 'It's nothing, really.' He could feel Adam's eyes shining on his back as he reached for another beer.

'He's named after Charlton Heston,' Rus said. Issy shook her head. 'He was an American actor, big in the '50s, '60s and '70s—'

'He started off open-minded,' Charlie cut in, 'a supporter of the civil rights movement. That's why my dad liked him. But he became very conservative, and was president of the NRA for a long time. A big fan of guns.'

Adam said, 'Nothing wrong with guns, mate. I'm sure you use them on your farm.'

Issy seemed to sense the rising tension. She changed the topic, asking Rus about his colours, as she often did. 'It still fascinates me. So, the valley is purple?'

'The big valley, yes,' Rus replied.

Issy moved on quickly, in that flickering way of hers. 'Do viruses have colours?'

'If they're named, they can. Same with cyclones, but only sometimes.'

'Do people?' Adam asked, leaning forward.

Rus smiled. 'Some do.'

'Give me some examples.'

'Issy's yellow, Grant's brown, and Charlie's gold.'

'What about me? Do I have a colour?'

Rus smiled again, this time with a little caution, perhaps. 'Adam is red.'

Adam nodded approvingly. 'Rus sees me as red.'

'No, the name is red.'

'So, the name always has the same colour?' Issy asked.

Rus now looked a little embarrassed, as if he'd been caught

out. 'No… it varies between people.'

'I *am* red, then!' Adam said triumphantly, and slapped Rus on the back. 'A strong heart, hey?'

They moved back towards more serious matters, back towards viruses and border closures. 'Keep that plane of yours in good condition,' Issy advised Adam. 'We might all need it one day.'

'I intend to, I promise you that.'

Rus had been quiet, but he watched Adam intently now.

'Just say the word, Isabel, and I'll fly you wherever you want to go, whenever you want to go.' Adam turned to Rus. 'And Rusty, we can escape whatever's coming.'

Rus smiled, but his eyes locked onto Charlie's.

'And you too of course, Chuck,' Adam said.

Charlie had previously corrected Adam's use of that diminutive form of his name, but he suspected a power play was in motion. He wouldn't feed it. Instead, he asked, without provocation in his voice: 'What about Grant? You can only fly four of us, right? Legally?'

'Legally, yep. But for the Cessna 172, it's really about weight. Besides, I think we'll enter a time soon when laws cease to exist.'

Charlie found that comment strangely disturbing. Issy laughed, and so did Rus.

Issy said, 'I can't imagine you ever being completely adherent to laws, Adam, regardless of the time.'

Adam shrugged, sipping his beer. 'But if it comes to it, Chuck, and it's between you and Grant, we can flip a coin.'

He reached over and rubbed Charlie's shoulder. It took all of Charlie's self-control to stop himself from recoiling.

THE VALLEY VI

The morning was bright, and the sky was clear. The soil remained sodden, but the signs were good – a burn-off might be possible in a few days.

Rus felt a slight remnant of last night. Not a hangover, but it was there, and he wished he could shake it. He considered the disturbances that played across his mind; it wasn't just alcohol that lingered. He pictured Charlie's face before bed, calm as it always was, but his dark eyes had been remote. Rus understood the source of that remoteness.

He tried the radio again. No Adam, but Issy was safe.

'Our radio's playing up,' she explained. She was as surprised by Adam's return, and by where he'd chosen to land, as Rus and Charlie were. 'I'll contact Audrey Aldis. She's gotten close to Adam recently.'

There were footprints, signs of crows around the yard, but not many. The night had passed without sounds of activity beneath the house.

'It makes me uneasy,' Rus told Charlie, as they completed a check of the place, more cursory than yesterday's. There was little to be gained from a thorough one, but they needed to make sure nothing significant had changed. It hadn't, not obviously. 'Like they're planning something.' The words, when spoken, sounded foolish. 'I know they aren't intelligent.'

'Then stop making them sound like they are.' Charlie shook his head, clearly perplexed. 'They hunt for food, warm themselves during the day, defend themselves against smart animals like us. They don't scheme. They don't plan our downfall or want our home. They're like saltwater crocodiles.'

'I know. I'm overthinking them.'

'You overthink everything.'

Ouch. But Charlie was right.

Saltwater crocodiles. Salties, as they called them in the north. Rus had never got used to the idea that such dangerous things lurked in the rivers and estuaries, or to the many *'Achtung'* signs that warned people of them. But the analogy was apt. Rus was sure he would never get used to crows either. *Don't overthink it,* he told himself.

They started planning for the burn-off, discussing how it would be done and what they would need. Around lunchtime, Issy made contact.

'Hey guys, I don't want to alarm you...' she said, through static, and of course it did, 'but I just spoke with Audrey. Her father heard from Adam yesterday. He radioed in to let them know he needed to land. He wanted to speak to Audrey, but John wouldn't let him.'

Issy took a deep breath. Even over the radio, even with her voice distorted, her hesitation was obvious. And ominous. Rus felt fear stirring again, adrenaline doing its work.

'Audrey said she was worried about her dad. Really worried. She said he wasn't acting normal.'

'Since when has John Aldis ever acted normal?' Rus asked. *Odd* didn't even come close to describing their neighbour. *Threatening* was a better word.

'I heard John in the background, yelling. Then the connection went dead.'

'Shit,' Charlie said. 'We've got to check in on them.'

Rus closed his eyes and nodded. He didn't like the Aldis family, didn't care for their wellbeing overall, just as they didn't care for anyone else's, but Audrey was blameless in this. She was the only good one in that family.

And Adam might be there.

'I was really hoping you wouldn't say that. I'm only telling you this so you know what's happening out there.'

Rus kept his voice calm. 'But we *don't* know what's happening out there, Issy.'

'And we owe it to them, we owe it to any survivor of this...' Charlie paused, seemed to look for the right words. 'This... *situation*.'

'Apocalypse,' Rus corrected him, but tried to make his tone light.

'Nah. It's not the end,' Charlie responded, seriously. 'There's no cascade failure yet. Systems correct themselves, the environment does.' His language had changed, country code shifting to academic.

Rus arched his eyebrows. 'Is that what this is? A correction?'

'I've started to think it might be, yeah. A global correction of *all* systems. Things may actually be better when it's all done.'

'Always the optimist, Charlton.'

Issy tried to dissuade their proposed expedition, but they were committed to it. They assured her they would take every precaution.

'You'll take guns?' she asked.

Charlie was quick to respond. 'Of course.'

'Guns can make things worse,' she said. 'That's what Adam says, anyway.'

'And sometimes they make things safer. Adam definitely *knows* that. We'll be fine, Issy. I promise.'

'We'll call you as soon as we get back,' Rus added.

Soon they were in the truck, heading down the small, pot-holed road that had once connected their property with a living world. It snaked through thickets of trees and scrub, over the river and into the northern section of the valley.

'I haven't been this far from our place in ages,' Rus said. 'It feels strangely normal out here.'

Everything was overgrown, but it was tranquil. Soothing, even. Fiddich sat between them, alert, excited at the adventure. Charlie drove. He always drove.

Reaching over, he patted Rus's knee. 'See? Environmental systems are repairing themselves.'

'Do the crows know that?'

A small laugh. 'They don't, but maybe they're helping in their own way, as scary as it might seem to us.'

They spotted a few crows as they drove, partly hidden by long grass, sugarcane and shrubs. Glimpses of ragged, watchful things. Arriving at the Aldis station, they stopped at the start of its driveway. Rus pointed at the 'No Trespassing' signs dotted about the property. 'They've always been very welcoming.'

'We've got a couple of those too. It's pretty common practice, since the virus hit.'

'We have *one*, and the Aldises had theirs years before the virus. John's always seen people like you and me as *trespassers* in this community.'

They got out of the truck. Locked it, at Rus's request.

Charlie pointed to the house. 'We'll walk slowly. Make

ourselves obvious. They know us, we should be fine.'

Rus put the lead on Fiddich. 'I'll keep him close. And hopefully quiet.'

'Make sure your gun's hidden,' Charlie said. 'We don't want anyone misreading our motives.'

'I should've baked a cake.'

Most of the cane fields had been burned or cut down low along the driveway and around the house. They could see the Aldises' airstrip clearly. No sign of Adam's Cessna; perhaps it was behind the house. There were remnants of burned crows – small mounds of flesh and fabric – but the death stench, when it came, was slight.

Close to the house, Charlie stopped abruptly. He pointed without speaking to another mound of crow, but this mound still burned, was in the final stages of burning, and sent up wispy fronds of smoke.

Rus looked to the house proper. Like theirs, it was raised from the ground, but it had multiple, broad stairways to its wide veranda. Most of them had been blocked by old fridges, cabinets, barbed wire. A small gap allowed entry towards the main door. That door was open.

'Not a good sign,' Rus whispered, and followed Charlie's lead, removing his revolver.

'It's Charlie and Rus,' Charlie called out. 'Everything okay in there?'

Fiddich whimpered. Rus raised a finger to his mouth and hissed a shushing sound. 'Are you *crazy?*'

'Noise doesn't wake the crows.'

'Not that we've experienced. Yet. Let's not test that theory here.'

There was no response from inside. The two manoeuvred

through the opening in the front steps. *It's an ugly house*, Rus thought. He'd always found it that way, but today it was even uglier.

Charlie pulled back the flywire door. It squeaked loudly, despite the care he took opening it. They entered the house.

Rus made placating signals to Fiddich. The dog was quiet, but his nose began to quiver, testing the air. It was silent inside, and the outside world felt suddenly very distant. The house was ugly inside too. A practical place, with no signs of comfort. No signs that it had ever been shaped to be more than a place to sustain life, basic life, even before life began to leave the world. It had never been a *home*.

The front rooms were empty. The main bedroom, a bathroom, another bedroom – all tidy, clean, harsh and empty.

'This is terribly wrong,' Rus whispered. The house felt like it had taken a deep breath and it held it in.

He led the way this time, wanting to find the end to this story quickly. He kept Fiddich close as he came out into the living room. But no one was living there now. Audrey Aldis lay dead on the floor. Her brother, Nicholas, lay close to the back door. Both were surrounded by pools of blood, dark, congealed to black.

'They've been shot,' he said, the shape that had been forming, the suppression of so much pain, so much loss, breaking through at last. His vision dimmed. The bodies before him were just things now, not people.

Audrey's wound was a deep void with ragged edges. Her forehead had been torn open by the blast, suggesting a close-range shot from behind. Nicholas lay on his front, arms outstretched, his lower back shredded by multiple wounds.

Charlie's voice was little more than a rasp. 'He was trying to get away.'

Rus felt sweat cling to him, cold. A metallic smell hung in

the air, the smell of drying blood and spent ammunition. As he turned, he caught sight of a boot. Made out the shape of a leg, protruding from the kitchen.

The body of John Aldis lay ruined on pale lino. The lino was splattered with red. The top of his skull had been ripped away, the gun still in his hand. Above him, the second hand on the kitchen clock ticked, covered in fragments of bone and brain.

Wind rattled the windows, as the house let out its breath.

CHARLIE II
THIRTEEN MONTHS AGO

The world was shutting down. Charlie and Rus had retreated to their farm. Everyone in the valley and ridge had done the same. Emergency broadcasts, while they were still active, delivered a simple message.

If you haven't left by now, don't. No assistance will come.

It was all happening with unexpected speed. The virus killed like nothing that had preceded it, spreading deadly tendrils over the land. Charlie could already predict the next phase. Soon, the structures of government would destabilise. Civic oversight and the protections it afforded would be abandoned.

At times, the emergency broadcasts were strangely vague. This worried Charlie more than what they explicitly outlined. The online chatter they triggered, intermittently now – there were no reliable connections – hinted at something else, at disastrous things unfolding within communities, undoing them, but there were no details.

Charlie and Rus worked about the house. Making it secure, shuttering up windows, watching for unexpected visitors. They maintained a façade of calm, but the pace they kept belied their urgency, their fear.

'We'll have to turn people away, even our mates,' Charlie said, 'until the virus burns itself out. Anyone could be a carrier.'

'What if it never burns out?'

'It will. But in the meantime, people will become desperate.'

'Unpredictable, selfish, dangerous,' Rus said, as he hammered nails into a window frame. 'The ugliness of our species is rising.'

'We have to be ready for it.'

'We're already becoming a part of it. We're shutting the world out.'

Anger flashed within Charlie. 'What do you suggest we do differently, Rus?'

'Nothing. I'm sorry, I just can't get my head around this. I still hoped humans could prove themselves to be better.'

'Not all humans are good. Wanting them to be good doesn't change that. And it doesn't mean our species has failed. Not yet.'

They continued their work in silence, Fiddich lying on the floor nearby, ears flat, picking up on the tension.

'How's the design for the stairs going?' Charlie asked.

'I'm an architect, not an engineer, but I think we can make it work.'

'We've got plenty of timber and tools. It might take a while, but we'll do it.'

They worked well into the night. By the time they were ready for bed, they found the broadcasts and information networks had fallen silent.

'It's great that you got the CB radio working,' Charlie told Rus. 'We've still got electricity, but now the phones are down, the grid probably won't last much longer. We need to work out alternatives.'

Rus sat at the end of their bed. 'Things might be better tomorrow.'

Charlie gave him a quizzical look.

Rus smiled. 'I'm trying to channel some of your optimism. I didn't sound very convincing, did I?'

'Nah, you didn't. But things *might* be. Let's get some sleep and see what the day brings. Coordinate with Issy and Grant and Adam.'

Rus stood and stretched, ready for bed. He focussed suddenly, intently, on Charlie. 'If things *do* get worse, if this is the end—'

'It's not—'

'—if it *is*, I'm really happy I'm with you, Charlie. Thank you. For everything.'

Charlie smiled, held the smile for a long time, held back stronger emotions. He sensed Rus was holding back something too. 'And?'

Rus stood there, his hair lightly tousled like he'd just styled it, his appearance immaculate despite the freneticism of their day, despite the humidity, the fear, the wrongness of the world. 'Nothing. I just... wish the world had had more time to change. For people like us.'

Charlie wanted to say something profound, offer words of comfort and love, but he was suddenly overcome by a need to protect Rus. To keep him safe from catastrophic events, and safe from people Charlie couldn't make sense of.

'Me too,' was all he could say.

THE VALLEY VII

Charlie stared out a window. Images of the Aldis family still burned in his mind. Bodies in distorted positions, no waking up, no coming back. Neighbours gone forever. They hadn't wanted to go, not the Aldis children.

Charlie and Rus were safe again in their house, but the sun was dropping fast and night creatures would soon roam freely. Rus prepared a quick meal. Neither of them had eaten since early morning, but they ate without vigour or conversation. Charlie glanced at Rus, felt Rus do the same to him, but neither held the other's gaze. Charlie didn't want to be human right now. He didn't want to deal with *his* human.

They finished their meal and cleaned up the kitchen with slow, deliberate movements. When they spoke, they spoke without emotion.

'We can't leave him out there,' Rus said, at last. 'Not with what we've just seen.'

Charlie stirred from his dark studies, his ruminations. 'No, we can't. But we can't go out now. We wait until morning, then we search, and we check on the Farley property. We owe it to them too.'

'It may already be too late. For Adam, I mean.'

'Maybe it is. But if he's alive, he'll take shelter. There are plenty of places for that in the valley. Crows aren't good at getting inside houses if you take the right precautions.'

'But they *can* get in, we've seen it before.'

Charlie nodded. 'What if…' It was an uncomfortable *what if*, but Rus saved him from completing it.

'What if Adam has the virus and passed it on to one of the Aldises?'

Again, Charlie nodded. 'It's a possibility. Why did John shoot his kids? Why did he shoot himself? Were they starting to change?'

'From what we've seen, it's not a rapid process. John would've had time to recognise the signs.'

'I wish we'd checked. We could've seen if they were becoming crows.'

'But we saw Nicholas. He'd been shot in the back, not the heart. And we know Audrey was scared when she spoke to Issy. Speech is one of the first things to go, so she wasn't changing either.'

Rus made good points, but Charlie wasn't completely convinced.

'John Aldis was always a cruel man,' Rus continued, with barely-concealed disgust. 'Domineering, even to his adult kids. I suspect it was an act of cowardice and violence and fear.'

'You're probably right. But we still don't know what triggered it. There must've been something.'

'We're back around to Adam, then,' Rus said.

'Perhaps tomorrow we'll find answers.'

'We need some. To plan, to make sure we can protect ourselves.'

You need answers more than me, Charlie thought. Back around to Adam.

RUS III
TWELVE MONTHS AGO

They drove to the Atherton Tablelands to pick up a generator, through farmland and hills, green pastures, knots of dense forest.

'I think we'll need it,' Charlie had said to Rus, when the borders started to close.

'That doesn't sound very hopeful,' Rus had responded.

'Just being safe, that's all.'

But Charlie didn't feel very hopeful either. The invocation of state powers, the raising of boundaries, no longer seemed like a means of protection. It seemed final. The last step before failure. There weren't many cars on the road as they drove down the coast, towards the hinterlands behind Cairns.

'Everything is brittle,' Rus said.

'What d'you mean?'

'The way people are talking, even the way they're driving.' The truck's windows were down, warm wind flooding the cabin, filling it with the smell of the sea. 'There's no confidence in things. It's like no one's sure anymore – they don't trust what they've been told, or they don't trust what they'll do if things get bad. And you can actually see it. Not in people's faces, but in the way they *are.*'

'True.' Charlie considered this. 'The other layers of life, eh, Rus?'

Rus grinned. 'So many layers.' And then, seriously, 'The layers are flattening out.'

Charlie turned to Rus, silently asking for an explanation.

'Every time the virus has changed, or we've been told the risk of infection is increasing, the layers have stayed in place. The way people see the world, the way they interact, the words they use, the meanings they give to everyday occurrences… all those layers have stayed in place.' Rus put his hand out of the window, let it drag the air. He grabbed at things absently, as if he were catching insects or snow. 'But now people are retreating to a simpler order of things, down to the base of Maslow's pyramid.'

'It makes sense to do that in times like these, doesn't it? What's the base level again? Physical needs?'

'And safety, yes. But we don't yet *know* this is a time of absolute crisis. We feel it, though.'

Charlie still wasn't ready to be honest about what he felt. Not with a man like Rus, who saw meaning everywhere. Instead, he asked: 'Does this particular time have a colour?'

'I think it does. I think it's white, a waiting colour, like *house* before it's a home. Or maybe I'm tapping into its symbolism, not its true colour.'

'You need to write a dictionary of colours and what they signify for me. I get lost.'

Rus laughed. 'I'll make a list and stick it to the fridge. But I get lost too, sometimes. Synaesthesia mixed with semiotics, colour signifiers and the signified… I'll do my best to bring order to it.'

They arrived in the town of Atherton. There were people on the streets, and they stared as Rus and Charlie's truck passed them.

'Suspicious,' Rus said.

'Concerned,' Charlie countered.

'Brittle, then. Ready to batten down the hatches.'

They turned off the main road and parked in the driveway of a house, its lawn strewn with car parts and what Rus described as junk.

'It's good to have people like Bob,' Charlie said. 'They've got a knack for salvaging and repairing things we need.' They needed the generator. They'd seen his ad for one on a community noticeboard, more reliable than the net these days. The generator was expensive, very expensive, but it was heavy-duty, and there weren't many available right now.

Bob was a surly man, not very talkative, but he said that people in the tablelands were preparing for the worst. When Rus asked him what that meant, he became silent. As soon as he was paid, he returned to the garage out the back of his place, leaving Rus and Charlie to lift the generator, all 150 kilograms of it, into the truck.

'I don't like that,' Rus said.

'He wasn't being rude. He's just got other things on his mind.'

'I didn't mean that. I meant that I don't like how people are becoming. The flattening out of things. Bob was flat. And this whole place is brittle.'

Charlie bit. He shouldn't have – he could read the signs, Rus was on edge – but he said: 'You're too sensitive sometimes, finding meaning where there's none.'

The day was hot, but Charlie felt the temperature in the truck drop.

'There's always meaning, or there should be,' Rus said icily, 'and we should look for it.'

'I don't think there is. I think we create it—'

'I know. *Life is meaningless, we all die, and we're all alone.* Your existential beliefs.'

Charlie bit back again. 'Whatever they are, they're my beliefs, and that's okay.'

'True. And so is finding meaning in things.'

'Finding and creating, they're two different things, Rus. And sometimes, we should just let things be. That's all I'm saying.'

'What if Bob was reacting to *us?* What if that was the reason for his sudden exit? He saw us as a threat to his way of life, not because of the virus, just because of who we are, and because he's gone back to the basics of his *being.* However that is for him.'

Charlie had considered the idea, but he'd dismissed it. There were other things to focus on right now. He hated to admit it, but he was also operating from lower in his own hierarchy of being.

They drove on in silence and in greenery, below a golden sun in an azure sky. They passed houses that showed efforts to augment protection. Small things, mostly. New gates, repaired fences, barbed wire. And sometimes, larger things – barricaded driveways, poorly-painted signs that promised violence to those who entered without invitation.

Charlie kept it to himself, but Rus was right. Everything was becoming brittle.

THE VALLEY VIII

Charlie slept surprisingly well. While Rus said he'd done the same, his eyes told a different story. Charlie hadn't heard much during the night, but Rus assured him the crows had been active. They packed additional supplies for the day – water, food, blankets, a first-aid kit – and headed back towards the Aldis property. Clouds sailed over the fields from the coast, not as dark as those from two days ago, but tinged with mauve, signalling that rain might come.

'I hope it holds off,' Charlie said, fingers digging into the leather of the steering wheel, body pressed close to it.

'God knows we need more drying time.' Rus angled his head towards Charlie. 'You're driving like your father, you know?'

'Shit. Things have really gotten bad, then.' Charlie pushed himself back in his seat.

They rolled up the Aldises' driveway, sounded the horn a few times, and got out of the truck.

'We should check inside,' Rus said, but hesitated at the steps. The smell of decay was strong.

'Probably means there are crows inside.'

Rus nodded. 'I'll check around the back. Maybe I'll be able to see in through the windows.' He started to move, and Charlie grabbed his arm.

'Not alone. We don't know this place.'

'I've got Fiddich,' Rus said, but his voice sounded uncertain. Then, 'You're right, not alone.'

The back of the Aldis house faced east, the opposite of their place. There were cane fields in the distance, but the area next to the house was neat and grassy. A Cessna sat there, gleaming white and blue when the sun broke through banks of cloud.

Charlie did what he knew Rus wanted to. 'Adam!' he called. A pair of masked lapwings standing on the grass responded in screeching voices and took to the wing, but Adam didn't answer, didn't come to the summoning. They waited, and eventually walked to the plane. It was secured, parked carefully by a tree. Not a crash landing, then.

'He's not here,' Charlie said, heading to the house.

'I know. Not alive, anyway.'

They checked the back windows. Most were boarded over, but they could see through slats into the living room. The two Aldis children still lay there. Their father's foot could just be seen. Nothing had changed.

Charlie tried to be pragmatic. 'Nicholas would be up by now if he was infected. We need to go.'

They left the cold property, with its cold story, and drove to Ballock Station. The Farley place was closer to theirs and usually had a much better feel to it than the Aldises' did. The driveway was winding, long, surrounded by cane, and scattered with crows. They counted five.

Charlie parked as close to the house as possible. The front door, entwined like the Aldises' in a barricade of wire and rubbish, was reassuringly shut.

'Let's make this quick,' Charlie said.

They stepped over obstacles designed to slow intruders, Charlie noted with disappointment, not to stop them. The front door was locked. The back door was locked too, and the windows were shuttered, so they could discern nothing from outside. They called to the Farleys but got silence in return. A familiar pattern was forming in their searches.

'We should force our way in,' Rus said. 'If we're wrong, you can fix the damage.'

'*I* can fix it?'

'You're much handier than me.'

Charlie forced the back door. It opened into a large room, a place of practicality, full of fridges and freezers, a carpentry table scattered with tools, and two heavy chairs that faced the back door. The walls were covered in tattered posters. By the door was a basket full of washing. It was hard to determine if its contents were yet to be taken out or had recently been brought inside.

'It smells like death,' Charlie said, almost gagging as he entered the house.

Rus covered his nose with his hand. 'I don't think there's much point in hanging around. There's no life here.'

Fiddich's ears lifted, and his nose started to twitch. In the dark, they listened.

'Can you hear that?' Charlie asked.

'It could be rats.'

'Rats don't make floorboards creak.'

'Big rats.'

Charlie headed into where the house became a home, a living room cluttered with colourful furniture, whimsical paintings and bright vases. There were photos too. Of children, grandchildren perhaps, and grey-haired people. A reminder of the first to go when the final outbreak struck.

The scraping sound continued.

Charlie moved towards the room it seemed to be coming from. As he peered through the door, a sharp gasping noise escaped him. He quickly cut it off.

A crow stood by the window, bathing in a puddle of afternoon sun. Silent, arms outstretched, head down, standing in the typical scarecrow pose. One of its hands flickered, hitting the side of a small table, making it creak. Charlie started to pull the door shut, carefully.

Fiddich lurched forward on his lead and barked. The crow turned. Its eyes remained closed, but it *looked* at Rus and Charlie. It started to shuffle towards them, made a sound like a sigh. They backed away. The door closed with a crisp click, a sound of safety and locking out bad things. But the bad thing behind the door struck at it and made it seem flimsy.

Charlie turned towards the front of the house. 'Let's go.'

They walked quickly to the truck.

'I reckon that was James Farley,' Charlie said.

'So who was the Farley lookalike standing in our field?'

'It would've been a bit of a walk for him to get to our place. This makes more sense. He must've locked the place up before he changed. And now he's stuck there. Kate's probably in there with him.'

'I hope Sara isn't.'

Charlie started the truck, and it spluttered to life in its usual way. Rus unclipped Fiddich from the lead. Before he could shut the door, the dog leapt out, barking, and disappeared into the cane fields.

They called to Fiddich for an hour, much longer than they'd called for Adam, but he wouldn't come back, or couldn't.

'We have to go,' Charlie said.

Rus stared at the swaying cane. 'He's alone in a field of crows. I can't go.'

Who is he referring to? Charlie wondered. *Adam or Fiddich?*

Charlie gently steered him back to the truck. He sat there, his face a forlorn mask, the energy he'd been drawing on now drained away. Important things had left him that day, had stepped off the edge of visible life. It seemed likely they would not step back.

CHARLIE III
TEN MONTHS AGO

Mossman was almost empty. Most of the shops were boarded over, had been for a few weeks now, but one of the town's two pubs was open. A last desperate attempt to keep things as they should be. An appeal for the town to be something else. It should've been a hopeful symbol, but Rus thought the darkness within made it look like the mouth of some creature, waiting to be fed. A guitar started to play from inside that mouth, an incongruently happy sound, a siren's song. *Enter, but beware.*

'It's like the Wild West,' Charlie said, as they walked along the street.

'Except that it's the tropics. We could order a pina colada from the *saloon*.'

'I'm tempted to go in there, for old times' sake.'

'There's a bad vibe coming from that place, Charlie. We should avoid it. Like we should've avoided coming here.'

'I just want to get a sense of what's happening, what we can expect, before we shut ourselves off.'

'You said you wanted to trade for more batteries,' Rus said.

Charlie sent him a guilty look, but said: 'Trade gives us a reason to talk to people.'

'Seeing as we're here, we should also check if there's anyone we can align with. We have Issy and Grant, Adam, maybe the Farleys, but it would be good to have more.'

'We don't need more.'

'We *do* need more, to make sure the future is okay.' Rus looped back to something Charlie had said just this morning. 'For us as humans, so our species doesn't return to the earth.'

Charlie ignored the layered meaning. 'I want to know how people might act if things go south.' Rus shot him a disapproving look, and he corrected himself. 'The south is a great place.' He winked. 'I mean if things go *bad*.'

Rus stopped walking, forcing Charlie to do the same. 'Things *are* bad. Really bad. You think they could get worse?'

'You don't?'

Rus did think things could get worse, but he had hoped, somewhere within his hidden thoughts, hidden even from himself, that Charlie held a different view. Rus trusted his own intuition, but he equally trusted Charlie's logic and Charlie's sense of how things *were*. Rus was more focussed on how things should be. He looked to illuminate problems when they came, found it difficult to deal with them as they were.

But Rus could feel his beliefs changing. People were changing, those who had caught the virus, and those who hadn't, in both cases into something new and bad. And Rus was starting to *flatten*.

They walked the main street, carefully, watchfully, but it remained empty. Behind them, when they were some distance from the pub, three people arrived on motorbikes. They glanced at Rus and Charlie and hurried inside.

'I think we should go into the pub,' Charlie said. 'Chat to people.'

'If you insist, but it's your shout, Charlton.' Rus considered this, shot Charlie a questioning look. 'Do they actually still *use* money here?'

'They're probably more likely to trade for things.'

'I doubt they deal in batteries.'

'If they deal in anything,' Charlie said, 'it'll be heavier stuff.' He rummaged around in his backpack and produced the remainder of the hospice kit. 'Which is why I brought some of Mum's drugs.'

Rus laughed. 'I thought you were saving them in case we needed them.'

'We do, but not for the reasons you thought we might.'

As they turned and started to walk back towards the pub, a voice called out, deep, resonant, loud: 'Hey! Rusty, Chuck!'

It was Adam. Charlie swung around to Rus and asked darkly: 'You *knew* he'd be here?'

'No.' Rus hesitated. He raised a hand to wave to Adam, then brought that hand to rub at the back of his head, suddenly self-conscious. 'I told him we were coming. He said he might be in the area.'

'But you didn't tell *me*?'

'Sorry,' Rus said, and he was, but not because Adam had arrived.

Adam sauntered over and patted them both firmly on their shoulders, a fluid, two-handed action, which Rus knew wouldn't sit well with Charlie.

'How are we doing, boys?' he asked, brightly.

Rus also knew Charlie hated being called that, *boy*, as if it somehow made him incomplete, a person yet to become. Rus wasn't taken by the title either, not unless it came from someone safe, but it came from Adam, and he was safe enough.

'How goes the battery hunting?'

Charlie shot Rus another dark look. Rus could see that he was controlling his responses. Noticed his jaw muscles flex, saw his eyes focus. Picked up on other things, just *sensed* them.

'You're the first person we've spoken to,' Charlie replied. 'We're heading into the pub—'

'Not a great idea,' Adam interrupted. 'It can be pretty wild in there. But with me here you should be fine.'

Charlie's face hardened. 'We can handle ourselves.'

'I'm sure you can – I didn't mean anything by that. Just safer in numbers is all, Chuck.'

Rus watched the interaction, wanted to intervene but knew that wouldn't help. He was glad Adam was here. He did feel lighter because of it, but it was more than that. Adam understood Rus, mostly, and he had an energy from which Rus fed.

Inside, the pub was lit by a harsh generator-powered light over the bar, and it was filled with people, at least twenty, murmuring quietly. In the corner sat the guitarist, now playing a melancholy tune. It took Adam to name it – *Paint it Black* – but it was familiar to Rus. They were inside the beast, and it didn't feel how Rus had expected it to. Charlie would have something to say about that if Rus admitted it to him, something about *expectations*.

Adam looked around. 'It's quiet here today.'

'Really? You come here often?' Rus asked, and instantly regretted it.

'Often enough, but not for much longer. It gets bad in here sometimes. And the alcohol's running out.'

They drank spirits, traded for them with supplies from the hospice kit, just as Charlie had planned. He was good like that, insightful; he saw things as they really were and could plan accordingly. They kept the 'heavier' drugs from the kit for some heavier trading if the chance presented itself.

Charlie seemed to relax. He spoke to a few of the patrons, if that term still applied, and he found the *sense* he was after. 'They see themselves as renegades, survivors outside the law. But not outlaws, not yet.'

'They're definitely outlaws, mate, by any definition,' Adam said. 'They're already dangerous, and they'll become worse when supplies run out.'

Charlie's posture became rigid again. But he nodded.

'Being an outlaw doesn't automatically make a person bad, though,' Adam added. 'Not if they follow their own rules, smart ones.'

Rus tapped his glass. 'It's the Wild West, just as you said, Charlie. Or the Wild North.'

Adam downed his drink, but had another lined up. They all did. 'It's worse further north, near the Daintree River. I've flown over what looked like barricades on the roads. I think I've spotted snares too.'

'That's disturbing,' Rus said. 'We've seen people near our place, wandering through properties. They don't seem threatening, only... lost.'

'People react in different ways,' Charlie said. 'We just need to keep up with what's happening, whether it's good or bad.'

They finished their third round. They had 'paid' for a fourth, and it slid down the bar soon after their glasses were empty. There was no risk of breathalysers anymore, and with the future uncertain, it seemed redundant to worry about drink driving.

Adam looked intently at Charlie. 'Chuck—'

'I prefer Charlie.'

Adam laughed. 'No worries, *Charlie*. I was going to ask...' He took a sip from his drink, held the moment. 'With your science background, what d'you make of how the virus is affecting people?'

Rus was pleased at the question; it might engage Charlie in the right way.

'That's not my type of science. I've got no idea what it does.'

Rus leant forward over the table. The guitarist was playing with gusto, improvising, or so Rus assumed, and the crowd was becoming louder. 'I don't think Adam's asking about virology,' he said.

Adam didn't wait for Charlie to respond. He said: 'When people first started to change, they were easy to deal with – we shot them, or stabbed them. The police and military did their part. But over time, they became harder to kill.'

Rus stared at his empty glass. 'And then the virus itself overwhelmed us. The police. The soldiers.'

'But we survived,' Charlie said, 'and we keep on surviving.'

The alcohol was unlocking things in Rus. It would be in Charlie and Adam too, although he suspected the keys to Adam's inner world were still out of reach. Lost, even.

'I don't know how we keep surviving,' Rus said. 'I don't know how we can even sit here and talk about it right now. We've seen so many things I never thought I'd have to see.'

'But we *are* alive, Rusty.' Adam spoke lightly. 'Chuck – sorry, *Charlie* – understands this better than most. It's enough. We're lucky.'

Charlie looked around at the people now laughing, now argumentative, now drunk, silhouetted in the dark pub. Rus knew he didn't need to find meaning from any of this. He and Adam were similar in that way.

'But getting back to my question,' Adam said, 'what's happening to the infected people now? I saw a few the other day near the river, in the bushes. It looked like they were *hiding*.'

Rus could see that Charlie's interest was piqued again.

'We've noticed something similar in the last few weeks,' Charlie said. 'They aren't standing in the open anymore. And they're not as active during the day.'

Adam shook his head. 'They're still fast when it suits them, though. Some idiots took shots at the ones by the river and got themselves killed. I went back the next day and there wasn't much left of the shooters. One of the creatures was lying there, too. The others had gone. They used to bleed when we shot them, but there was no blood, just... it looked like yellow oil seeping from the wounds, and it fuckin' stank.'

Rus screwed his face up involuntarily. 'You shouldn't go near them, Adam.'

'I know. I kept my distance, in case it came back to life. But like Charlie, I want to know what I'm up against.'

'I don't know what we're up against,' Charlie said. 'But you're right, they're changing. I'm not sure why. They're very different to the first ones we saw. Much harder to kill, and that's something we should keep in mind. They might not be *human* anymore, but they are alive. And their death is final.'

Adam's attention intensified on Charlie. He leant in closer and said: 'See, you do have ideas about them. Is there anything more?'

The guitarist now sang *Hurt*, managing a good impression of Johnny Cash. It matched the mood of the place, even of the time.

'No, nothing solid,' Charlie said, without conviction.

'Tell Adam what you told me this morning, Charlie.'

Charlie hesitated, looking uncomfortable, but relented. 'I was just talking out loud. It's a half-formed idea, but... what if the human species is an evolutionary accident, and it's failed? And what if the genetic evolution that allowed us to develop complex cells was caused by viruses, and now it's being undone by viruses? Maybe humans are…'

'Humans are what?' Adam asked.

'I don't know. Going back to the land?'

Adam laughed. It surprised Rus. It was surely not intended to be patronising, but he wished Adam had responded differently.

'Maybe we *can* have it all,' Adam teased, lining up skilfully with the guitarist's lyrics. 'Their *empire of dirt,* when people are all gone.'

Charlie smiled thinly, finished his drink, and said: 'Like I said, it's a half-formed idea. There's probably nothing in it.'

Rus wasn't too sure. It was where Charlie differed to Adam – Charlie's thinking wasn't purely linear. *Is this illumination?* he wondered.

He tried to distract from Adam's reaction. 'It's the thing I'm most scared of, to be honest.'

'We all go back to the earth, Rusty. Everything goes away in the end!'

'That's not what I meant.' But Rus chose to say no more. Unlike Charlie, he accepted Adam's nickname. It was one he'd worn before, and it matched his colour for Icarus. Symbolism combined with intrinsic association.

Charlie looked at Rus, almost apologetically. 'I'm not sure if I think it's bad. The natural world is fixing itself, finding ecological balance. It's not a popular theory anymore, but maybe that's what it is.'

Again, Adam laughed. This time, it did sound patronising. 'I don't buy into any of that *nature balance* crap. It's chaos theory in action, plain and simple. We just need to kill every fucker who's been infected, provide a bit more chaos, then rebuild. People like us should take the lead.'

The pub became louder still. The click of pool balls, the sound of the guitar, the smell of cigarettes, the drunken talking and shouting; it was simultaneously normal and foreign, comforting and terrifying, for reasons Rus couldn't define. A middle-aged man, burly, bearded and incredibly intoxicated, staggered into Rus, knocking his drink from his hand. It shattered on the floor.

Adam's reaction was swift. He grabbed the drunken man by his T-shirt, held it in a clenched fist that looked ready for more than just holding, pushed the man heavily against a wall.

'You owe my friend another drink,' Adam said, his tone velvety. Cheerful, even. 'You'll get him one, right?'

The drunken man nodded, mumbled, 'Sorry, mate,' and turned to leave.

'We could all do with another round,' Adam called after him. 'Whisky, this time. The water of life.'

He nodded a second time. Adam could do that. Manoeuvre people, bend them to his will.

Adam smiled at Rus and Charlie. 'That was no accident,' he said to them.

Rus wasn't sure. It had felt like an accident, but when he looked at the burly man's friends standing near the bar – one small but full of menacing energy, the other bland and self-satisfied – he thought perhaps he did see *something,* a look of hatred, more than just anger. Maybe it was directed at Adam, maybe it was caused by Rus and Charlie being who they were, where they were. Maybe it was a mixture of both.

'You stand out way too much here, Rusty,' Adam said.

'Story of my life.'

They got the round of whisky that Adam had 'asked' for, and he became light-hearted, regaling them with anecdotes that were humorous, distracting, and largely forgettable. Charlie, on the other hand, became quiet and watchful. Rus had no doubt that he could defend himself if needed – his build was strong, different to Rus's lean physique – but fighting would be his last resort.

Adam seemed more than ready for violence if it should come. He'd repositioned himself to stand, so he could scan the pub. He seemed calm, so calm, but Rus could see his thumb, the one that held his drink, tapping and flicking the glass. And his knuckles, when his fingers fully engaged, were white – he held the glass with a grip that might break it. He was a spring now, tightly wound, and Rus found himself strangely concerned about what would happen if that spring were to snap.

Adam's eyes tracked the burly man and his friends as they headed outside, but he kept the conversation jovial and constant. They finished their drinks and left the pub. Adam called a cheery farewell.

Rus blinked. Although the light was fading, it jarred with the shifting darkness inside. It reminded him of leaving a daytime movie in a backstreet cinema and returning to the real world, those simple surreal joys of his life before.

Adam headed towards his car, Rus and Charlie towards their truck. Its doors were open. Two men rummaged through the interior. There was little for them to find; anything of value was in Charlie's backpack.

Charlie spoke, his voice tinged with anger and surprise. '*Fuck off* – that's our stuff.'

The men were out of the truck in a heartbeat. One was the burly man from earlier, the other his friend with menacing energy. The friend was gaunt and carried the look of a hunted animal.

Rus put a hand across Charlie, tried to create a barrier to prevent him from proceeding, but he pushed through it. They had discussed bringing weapons before coming here. Rus had dissuaded the idea, said it wasn't needed.

The attackers *did* have weapons: the hunted man had a

machete, an extension of the anger and threat in his eyes, and the bigger man produced a smaller knife. It glinted in the dull light.

Rus scanned quickly for objects of protection or defence, his default for flight switching to fight, without thought or reasoning. Charlie was doing the same; he scooped up a piece of metal from the road.

Adam appeared behind the two attackers. He strode towards them silently, a broken, amber beer bottle in his hand. Rus saw the colour and the symbolism that might form later. Adam stabbed the smaller man in the side of the neck, twisting the jagged glass slightly, then a second jab, this time into the front of his throat. There was a gurgling sound, high-pitched and full of surprise, blood pumping onto the road in spurts. The machete fell.

Charlie moved for the larger man. Rus saw it, delayed, in his head – slow movement coloured by twilight, bright red on brown dust and black asphalt. Rus moved to follow, but already Adam was there, kicking away the small knife and deflecting blows from the big man with ease. Adam soon had him on the ground. Pummelled his head with massive fists, then lifted and smashed it, again and again, onto the road.

Rus almost marvelled at the simple collapse of skull and flesh, the exposure of things not supposed to be exposed. The quietness of the counterattack, the quickness of death. The cicadas. The twisted intimacy.

When it was done, Adam stood motionless, breathing heavily. He stared at his bloody hands, held them high, and laughed. In his calm voice, he said: 'Out, damned spots. Out.'

He smiled at Rus and Charlie, but the smile quickly vanished. He pointed back towards the pub – patrons were emerging, among them the self-satisfied friend.

'We've gotta go, *now.*' Charlie pushed Rus towards the still-open truck. 'Get in,' he said to Adam, but Adam turned back the way he'd come.

'Don't come back here, boys. It's really not safe for you,' Adam called, then sprinted away into the darkening evening.

The world was never truly safe, but some places were safer than others. Rus still managed to work in layers. His thoughts gained speed, perhaps even clarity, despite what had just happened: he heard advice, words of insight. Adam was capable of that much. That place was not safe anymore. The music and drinks had played with Rus's perception, and he and Charlie could've ended up dead today.

Perhaps it never had been safe. Not for *boys* like them.

THE VALLEY IX

The house felt empty, even to Charlie, and the land did. A strange, diffused light had come over the place, the last of the sunshine mixed with clouds, wistful and heavy. *Rus is rubbing off on me,* Charlie thought, and decided that wasn't a bad thing.

Charlie went about his preparations for night-time. He secured the house, closed the few open shutters, raised the bridge with Rus. He almost went to put food into Fiddich's bowl but caught himself. He kept seeing Fiddich's shape in the deepening shadows.

There is no meaning in that, he reminded himself, and yet found he wanted meaning right now. He needed to recreate some, for both of them, he decided. Tomorrow he would, or next week. Charlie's way of being, merging with Rus's. It was a strange thing.

Rus spoke very little. Charlie followed his lead, not that he had much to say. Neither touched Adam's whisky, each for his own reason, unspoken to the other. For Charlie, it seemed crass, to drink Adam's gift when the man was out there, maybe, trying to survive the night.

Charlie joined Rus on the front veranda. They watched the last of the sunset without words, not needing them, or not capable of them. But as time wore on, Rus's silence began to worry Charlie. He was breaking. He was flat, not only in the affective sense, but *flat* by his own definition of such things. For him, survival was all that existed right now. Charlie could live with that, had lived with it for a long time, but he couldn't continue that way when Rus needed more and there was nothing more left.

'We'll get through this,' Charlie said.

'I know.' Rus's response was listless.

Charlie watched the last light fade. Vibrant colours left the sky, clouds thickened in the distance; there might be another storm. Vespertine creatures moved in the twilight and Charlie knew that the crows would be waking. Everything else was still. He loved this time of day, or usually did. He loved the solitude, had embraced the receding of human interaction – as terrifying as the source of it was – but recently, he'd observed the greater loss this could bring.

Rus is definitely rubbing off on me.

ISSY II
NINE MONTHS AGO

Rus walked with Issy through the little valley. The place radiated green, not just in colour, but in the feel of it, much deeper than mere verdant tones, and it was tinged with gold.

'It's a bit like home,' he told Issy. 'Like the valleys outside Hobart.'

'Slightly warmer, I imagine,' she said, holding a mug of peppermint tea.

'Yeah, just a bit.'

Charlie was with Grant, over in the old house. They were talking station stuff, things that Rus tried to learn about, was improving his knowledge of, but to which he still had little to contribute.

'It's good for them to just be *farmers* with each other,' Issy said. 'When we're with them, they have to explain things to us.'

Rus nodded. 'They're lucky. They both have remnants of the old times; you and I have none of that.'

'I don't think I need it, not in the same way as you.'

'I wish I could be like you, Issy.'

She laughed. 'I don't think you should.'

'You fit in so easily—'

'Is that what you think?'

She looked genuinely surprised, and Rus suddenly wondered if he'd said something terribly insensitive. 'Have I got that wrong?'

'I don't know. Maybe I make it look easy. But I always feel like I stick out – much like you. Here in North Queensland, back home in Tromsø even, especially when I was a teenager. I looked different to my school friends. My mum's ways were very different, and so were some of mine. They still are. I've made peace with that, but it doesn't mean it's not hard sometimes.'

'I'm sorry. I didn't think—'

'It's okay, Rus, truly.' She hugged him, a warm hug that mirrored her words. 'I value your difference, and I know you value mine. And perhaps mine's what makes me so restless sometimes, just as yours makes you want to go home to the south.'

'It's tricky business, this fitting in, this blending,' Rus said, and laughed. The laughter was at himself.

'Blending in is sometimes just camouflage,' Issy said.

The two walked on, waterlogged patches of ground squelching underfoot.

'Still, I'm glad Charlie and Grant have each other,' Rus said, still not quite ready to leave it. 'They can talk about things other than the stations – they've got high school memories, so many shared experiences.'

'They were never really close growing up, from what Grant tells me. And you've got Adam and me. It's why I introduced you to Adam. I knew you two would hit it off.'

They stopped at the banks of a muddy dam, holding their mugs of tea while welcome swallows skipped over the water, dipping into it, causing intricate ripples, catching tiny insects.

'Adam...' Rus sighed.

'You're still disturbed by the other week.'

'Wouldn't *you* be? He killed two men in front of us.'

'And those men would've killed you and Charlie.'

'Don't let Charlie hear you say that.'

Issy lowered herself onto a small boulder. Rus joined her. The sun glinted on the water and Issy's dark hair. Like Rus, she wore sunglasses; they inclined sharply and gave her an elfin look.

'Adam saved us, I know.' Rus sighed again. 'It's just how he did it.'

'He's ex-military, what do you expect? He improvised.' Issy spoke with Charlie's pragmatism. And Adam's.

'It made me wonder about his past. Do you know much about it?'

'I promised Adam I wouldn't talk about it.' Issy swatted at a large mosquito that had landed on her arm.

'Having context would help. Charlie's still unsettled by the whole thing too.'

'I'll say this – Adam's what the army made him. I don't think it's fair to punish people because of conditioning. If we make people, then we have to live with the good and the bad in them.'

'So, there *is* something bad in his past?'

'Adam did what he had to do, using the skills he was trained in. I don't see any problem with that.'

'Are you talking about the other week in the pub, or something else?'

'I really think you should drop it, Rus. Adam's a good man; let that be enough.'

'I want it to be enough. I like him, but I know Charlie doesn't.'

'As you just said, Charlie has Grant.'

Rus furrowed his brows but gave a quick nod. It wasn't quite the same thing. 'You *do* think Adam is good, whatever that means, don't you?'

'He wouldn't be in my circle of friends if I didn't,' Issy shot back.

'I'm not too sure about that,' Rus said, smiling. 'I never picked Grant as your type.'

'Don't let Grant hear you say that.'

Frogs began to call in the reeds on both sides of the dam. One group would start, the second would answer.

'And what is my *type?*' Issy asked suddenly.

'I think you secretly like the dangerous ones.'

Issy laughed. 'That's no secret.'

The frogs continued their echolalic singing. The afternoon deepened.

'In answer to your question,' she said, 'yes, I think Adam is good. I think he has a moral code. It's different to yours and mine, but it's there. And he's more complex than he lets on. You caught a glimpse of that – that's all.'

Rus drained the last of his tea. The sun's warmth was reassuring, as were Issy's words. 'Thanks, Issy. I feel better about it all.'

Issy smiled at him. 'In times like these, we need people like Adam.'

The swallows continued to swoop; they caught more insects with clicking beaks. In a blur, they retreated to the brilliant blue sky, leaving no signs that they had ever hunted over this water, brown and still, noisy with frogs.

ADAM II
THREE WEEKS AGO

Rus sat beside Adam in his Cessna as it climbed above the fields. The ground fell away, and bright greens and deep blues stretched out around them. Adam banked the aircraft and pointed out Rus and Charlie's place. Charlie would hear the plane, and Rus felt bad for that. Still, he felt lighter than he had for some time. Leaving the ground meant leaving the danger, the horror, at least for a while.

Adam steered towards the coast, kept largely to a course that tracked the division between land and water, flew high enough to avoid projectiles – he said his plane had been shot at before – but low enough to see the world. 'It's safer this way,' he explained.

For a long time, Rus just stared out at the scenery. 'I feel like a tourist,' he said.

'I'm glad the tourists are gone,' Adam replied. 'They were annoying.'

But Adam pointed out a few places of note, assumed his tour guide disguise with ease. He spoke of the beaches, the bluffs, the flora and fauna that lived below, showed sincerity where apparently there was none.

Silence fell again for a time. Just the steady sound of the plane's engine, the warmth of the sun through the window, the unfolding of scenery.

Adam broke it. 'I'm surprised Chuck let you come on this trip.'

Rus became instantly guarded. 'Charlie didn't *let* me do anything. We agreed it was valuable – we might learn something new. And he's doing security maintenance, otherwise he'd be here instead of me.'

'Let me put it another way, then. I don't think Chuck likes me very much.'

'He hates it when you call him Chuck. I don't like it either.'

'Sorry,' Adam said lightly.

'You don't do much to make Charlie like you.'

'Am I supposed to?'

'It would make our friendship easier.'

'Then what can I do, Rusty, to make it… easier?'

'Charlie's careful by nature. He's wary about things outside his realm, especially when it comes to this place, his home ground. It's the only time I've seen him be protective. Not of me, rarely of me, but of the things that are important to him.'

'I'd say that's mostly you. I've tried to break through, but he doesn't want me to.'

Rus could see Adam's subtle choreography again, the way Adam *worked* people.

'He can be difficult to crack, sometimes, but if you try, you'll get there. It's worth it.'

Rus wanted to tell Adam the truth: that Charlie likely thought it was too dangerous for anyone to get close to him. But perhaps this would feed into his vanity, a vice that he carried, like so many men. He concealed it as carefully as he could, but Rus caught glimpses of it.

Adam kept his eyes on the horizon, his mouth closed. Rus could see the slightest hint of a smile on that closed mouth. It forced Rus to speak. More manoeuvring. 'I think Charlie reacts to what you represent.'

Before Adam could respond, a glint below drew Rus's attention. Their flight path largely aligned with the main road that connected Mossman with Cairns. It was empty, or Rus had assumed it was, but now he could make out a car driving along it.

'Fuckwits,' Adam said. 'They're heading to Cairns.'

'So are we.'

'But we won't go into the city. We won't land.'

'Do you see many cars when you fly?'

'More than you'd expect. Not at first, but things have settled down a bit. There's a kind of normality to life down there, or it looks like that from up here, sometimes.' Adam paused, his mouth curling further. 'So, tell me, what *do* I represent, Rusty? Or do I need to call you Icarus?'

'I've told you before, I'm fine with Rusty. I got called that at uni sometimes. Rus or Icarus are fine too. Just stop using Chuck, okay?'

'Sure, mate. But back to my question…'

'I don't know exactly what you represent, Adam. Flight. Escape. Something along those lines. Just symbolic stuff, that's all. Charlie thinks I want to be alone with you, but I don't.'

'It's the Cessna you love,' Adam said, with a laugh.

Rus smiled in spite of himself. 'True. But I like that you understand being an outsider here. And I enjoy your company.'

'Me too. I'll keep trying to crack *Charlie,* for your sake. Any tips?'

'He's perceptive. He knows you don't care much for him.'

'Is that what you think?'

'I think so, Adam, yes.'

'I care about his partner, though.'

'That may be part of the problem.'

Adam winked. 'Got it. Flirt with him more.'

'Definitely not; that's not the way to Charlie.' Rus became more serious. 'He may think you're a bit of a closed book—'

'And he *isn't?*'

'Point taken. You're similar in that way. But you know a bit about his life just by being here. Maybe give him something more.'

'And you don't need that? Something more?'

Rus thought about that for a moment. 'Maybe. Depends what you mean, I guess. I'd like to know a bit about your life before you came to the north, but Issy warned us not to ask about your military past. That makes me avoid asking questions.'

'Everyone has a past, Rusty, and everyone has something from it they'd rather not talk about.' Adam's posture stiffened. His hands gripped the plane's yoke with white knuckles. It reminded Rus of the way he'd held his whisky glass on that distant violent day, inside the Mossman pub.

'I suppose that's true. I don't *need* to know more.' It was a lie, but Rus said it as much for himself as he did for Adam. Still, Adam's past, his capacity for violence, weighed upon Rus. 'I only need your plane,' he added, with a lightness that mirrored Adam's. Manipulate the manipulator.

It worked, to a degree. Adam's posture relaxed, as did his hands. He asked, without looking at Rus, 'If you weren't avoiding asking me questions, what would you ask?'

He was strangely open. Still guarded, still careful, but Rus had an in. Perhaps it was because they were in Adam's domain, and Adam controlled everything up here. Rus doubted he would get another chance, and this openness would probably only exist for one question. One. He had at least two big questions, and scrambled to decide which one would offer him the most insight.

'That day at the pub,' he said, slowly, 'did you have to kill those guys?'

Adam exhaled, sharp and explosive. 'Are you serious? They would've fuckin' murdered you two. I can't believe you've been holding onto this.'

Taken off-guard, Rus felt an urgent need to soften things. 'Sorry, Adam. I haven't been holding on to it, really. But even with what I've seen since the world went to shit, that was pretty confronting.'

Adam breathed in deeply. His voice became flat. 'What's the question you want to ask me, Rusty?'

Rus looked at Adam, confused. 'That's it. That's my question.'

'Nah, that was an insinuation. If you're going to question my fucking motives, then be upfront about it – what do you want to know?'

Rus scrambled to push his advantage, however fragile it now seemed. Adam almost had him in retreat, but there were levers to this conversation. And Rus hoped he'd found the fulcrum.

'Okay, then, fair point,' he said, as if backing off. 'I know as a solider you're trained for combat. Trained to kill.'

The plane's propeller blades blurred before him; slight turbulence buffeted the aircraft.

'Do you enjoy it?' he asked, keeping his voice low and even, not taking his eyes off the blades.

Adam laughed loudly. 'Much better question. Now you're being honest!'

'And?'

'I enjoy using the tools of my trade.'

'You wanted honesty and clarity,' Rus said. 'Give me the same. Killing is one of the *tools of your trade*; do you enjoy using it?'

'I like all the tools I've got at my disposal. I keep them sharp, and I use them to remove any impediments I find.'

'That's still ambiguous.'

'Then you're being a bit thick, mate.' Adam ruffled Rus's hair, a strange show of physical familiarity in the middle of such dark revelations. 'It doesn't make me a bad person.'

Adam sounded like he was channelling Issy, or she had been channelling him when Rus spoke with her in the little valley.

'Life's always been about survival,' Adam said. 'Way before the crows came.'

He sounded like Charlie again, driven by forces that Rus appreciated, but that lacked the meaning Rus wanted them to have.

Adam continued: 'My job was, still is, about making sure the right ones survive, that's all.'

Rus saw it. A glimpse of Adam's strange code, the dark compass that guided him. It was very different to Rus's code, or Charlie's, but Issy was right. It existed. Rus considered himself good at reading others, sensing their motives, understanding why they behaved as they did. But a glimpse was as much as he could get into Adam's mind.

He wanted to know more about how Adam worked, how he formed his decisions, but they were reaching the outskirts of Cairns. Rus could *sense* that the way to that understanding was shut again, at least for now.

Adam confirmed it by changing topics. 'That day at Issy and Grant's, when you were talking about your and Charlie's namesakes...'

Rus felt his defences coming up.

'Charlie cut you off – what were you going to say?'

God, he's quick.

'I said it.'

'Nah, you didn't, Rusty. It's fine if you don't want to tell me, though.'

Rus sighed. It wasn't a big secret or anything; he wasn't sure why Charlie had stopped him telling it at the barbeque. 'I was going to say that his dad's favourite Charlton Heston movie was *The Omega Man*.'

'Ah, yeah, a solid movie. Why would Charlie care about that?' A pause, and then, 'Heston played the last man to survive after a war. Charlie doesn't like that connection, is that it?'

For the second time, Rus thought: *God, he's quick*. Now he regretted giving that small secret.

'Technically, he wasn't the *last* man alive,' Rus said, a correction that Charlie would've made.

'Either way, I can't really see it. Charlie at the end of all things.'

Adam didn't speak with any judgment in his voice, but it annoyed Rus. 'I can't see it for any of us,' he said, and folded back into the silence, angry that he'd said too much.

Adam circled the small city. It was more a big town, by Rus's definition of things. Adam steered low over the streets, sweeping above the grid matrices that made up the place.

'I'm not really sure what I expected.' Rus spoke quietly, distracted by being back in *civilisation*. 'The buildings are still standing. Nothing seems to have been burned out. And the cars are all neatly parked.'

'I thought the same thing when I first flew over here. I was expecting a disaster zone, total destruction, but it's not like that.'

'It looks like it's early in the morning and the world hasn't woken up yet. It looks peaceful.'

'From what the people in the tablelands tell me, it's not. There are crows everywhere, but they're hiding in the buildings. And they're more active here, or so I've heard. They attack in daylight.'

Adam dipped the plane lower. Rus could see them then, in the doorways, under street trees. So many scarecrows, largely concealed but still seeking the sun. 'Why do they stay in the town? There's no food for them here.'

'Rusty, you've just asked the million-dollar question. If we answered that, we'd understand something important about them.'

They searched from above but found nothing of value. Adam flew them to the airport. A single jet sat on the tarmac. There were plenty of light aircraft, though: a few small propeller passenger planes and some helicopters. That was the other part of this mission – to work out if it was safe to land there.

'Could you fly any of them, other than the Cessnas?'

'The helicopters, yeah. Maybe one of the passenger planes if I gave myself time to work out their instruments. But I don't plan to.'

Rus asked, half-knowing the answer already, 'Then what's the point in coming back here?'

'There's plenty of fuel down there. For when I leave.'

Rus was suddenly conflicted. There was a sense of impending loss – another person important to him might be leaving. But it might make things easier in some ways.

'And when do you think that'll happen?' Rus asked.

'Not sure. Soon enough.'

'Where will you go, Adam?' As Rus said the name, he saw that its colour was changing. It was still red, but not as bright as it once was.

'South, like we talked about.'

'That was never serious.'

'Yeah, it was, Rusty. It was.'

Adam tapped a dial in the cockpit, concentrated on his plane, before he spoke again. 'It's the temperate marine climates that are the safest during end times, apparently, especially temperate marine *islands*. Ireland, Iceland, New Zealand…'

Rus knew what was coming.

'And Tasmania. That's where I'll head, see how far I get. And anyway, I can't stay here anymore. It's time to move on.' Adam turned his gaze towards Rus, those green eyes working their strange influence on him, making him attentive. 'You can come with me, if you want.'

Rus was disturbed by Adam's reason for leaving. He wanted to ask what made it time to move on, but held back.

'So will you come?'

He was flattered; he couldn't hide from that fact. He was suspicious, too. And the southern promise no longer worked on him, not in the same way. Rus had played that game before – a cruel one, even if it had just been a game of words. He wouldn't play it anymore.

'With Charlie,' he said, testing Adam. 'And Issy and Grant.'

'Limited room, Rusty. There are choices we'll have to make.'

'Then the answer's easy. No.'

'I'll check in on you before I leave. The invitation stays open.'

Rus wanted to say he wouldn't change his mind, but he said nothing.

They circled the airport a few times, didn't see any crows, and decided it would be safe to land. Another mission, for another time, if Adam stayed long enough.

The colour of *Adam* continued to change. That happened

occasionally, the colour of names developing and shifting over years. But this process was rapid. The plane pierced the shimmering blue sky, and the colour of Adam's name clouded.

THE VALLEY X

Lightning flickered throughout the night. It hovered over the horizon, starting before Rus and Charlie went to bed. They could see it from the front veranda, dry lightning over the land, perhaps accompanied by rain out to sea. It sent rumblings to shake the house, which would've been oddly soothing, except that Fiddich was out in it.

It was just after 5 a.m., and Rus lay awake. He knew from Charlie's breathing that sleep had left him too. When the light finally came back, Rus said, 'He was out there alone all night.'

Charlie didn't respond, so Rus clarified: 'Fiddich. He should've been with us. He must've been terrified.'

'I know.' Charlie's voice was kind. 'He's a smart boy – he'll probably find his way home.'

A sense of loss hung over Rus this morning. It pressed against his chest and kept him in bed, even when he should've been doing his checks. Charlie was already out of the house by the time he pushed the heaviness away, but it didn't go far. He secretly hoped that Charlie would come back in and bring Fiddich with him.

When Charlie did return, he was carrying two cups of coffee. The usual ritual, made with a small fire in the brick barbeque.

'Thanks,' Rus said, and sipped the hot drink. Cicadas were

already singing. 'What's the plan today?'

'The same as always. To survive.' Charlie's voice had an edge to it. That was unexpected, and rare.

Rus heard his own voice harden, something not so rare. 'I mean, should we look for Fiddich or get on with the burning?'

'Still too wet to burn. We could look for Adam.'

That stung a little. Was Charlie finally bringing things out into the open? Rus let it go. *Don't overthink things.*

Rus picked up a framed photo of Charlie's parents. He wasn't good with the rustic aesthetic, or with framed photos, but when he'd moved into this house he had accepted both. He found strange delight in these reminders of another life. In the photo, Charlie's parents sat together on a couch, holding hands, smiling. 'I really like this photo.'

'Me too.'

'I'll try Issy this morning. I'm sure it's nothing, but the lack of contact yesterday bothers me.'

'Their unit's probably playing up again. Though I would feel better if you could get onto them.'

Rus finished his coffee. 'I've been thinking. Maybe we should get out of here, find another place—'

'Our place is safer than any we know of.'

Crossing his arms, Rus asked: 'Is any place really safe?'

'What do you want me to say, Rus?' There was still anger in Charlie's voice, but it had lessened. 'The world has become a different place, and you're right, nowhere's safe. How does that help?'

Rus's own anger rose quickly. 'You sound like Adam.'

Charlie stood at the sink, looking down. 'I'd prefer you didn't compare me with him, but yeah, sometimes we think the same.'

He poured out the rest of his coffee. 'And I can't keep trying to make this place home for you.'

'What are you talking about?'

Charlie placed the empty mug in the washing-up crate, to be taken out to the tank later.

Rus's anger grew, his resentment, that *shape* almost fully formed. 'Everything is pointless. Being here, trying to keep going.' He wanted to hurt Charlie with his words, hated himself for wanting it. The sequence was starting again, and the off switch seemed broken, as it often was when his emotions ran hot.

Still not looking at Rus, Charlie said, 'There's always a point. But I can't make you see it.' More silence, then: 'If Adam ever asks you to go south with him, I want you to seriously consider it.'

Rus was horrified by the suggestion. He let his expression convey that.

'I want what will work for you, Icarus. I really do.'

Cicadas sang, but otherwise, it was too silent.

'No,' Rus managed to say, at last. 'I'd never do that. I want to help, I want to be here for you.'

'For me or *with* me?' This time it was Charlie who moved away, heading towards the back door. Patient Charlie, beautiful Charlie, the man who indulged Rus when he went white – not the colour of waiting people, days and places – but the colour of deep rage, of lashing out.

'I'll get more eggs for breakfast,' was all Rus could say, as Charlie walked away from him. *Change this. Be that charming man he once imagined.* Breakfast, the word, was gold, and that colour was important, but Charlie didn't know it. Rus had never made that dictionary.

Rus went out to the chicken coop. He replayed the conversation, over and over, both angry and regretful at what lay behind it, on both sides. But the fact they still argued comforted him. *We're still human. We still get caught up in simple things.*

The hens made contented sounds as he approached them. They weren't far from the coop; out at first light, no doubt. They pecked at something in the drying mud.

As Rus approached, he recognised what it was. A fingernail, whole and intact. Nearby, shreds of skin and organs lay scattered across the yard.

ISSY III
TWO WEEKS AGO

The trees on the ridge created a radiant green canopy, blocking out some of the heat. Beneath that canopy, Rus and Charlie sat on the deck of Issy and Grant's house, a breeze bringing relief from the blazing day. Issy's two dogs played with Fiddich on the small grassy area before the deck. Rus liked it here. The house was modern, all glass and sleek lines and touches of wood, with polished concrete floors and louvre windows. Issy had designed its build. The original farmhouse was still there, down in the little valley, and Grant often spent nights in it to make his farming duties easier. Up here on the crest of the ridge, though, there were hints of sophistication, architectural appreciation, the airy sense of home and the colour that came with that word.

Issy handed cold drinks to her two guests. 'The old season has ended. A new one has begun.' She skilfully reflected Charlie's metaphor back at him. 'This thing that's come our way is here for a long time, I believe. It'll pass eventually, but for now, we're the ones who must adapt.'

'I agree,' Charlie said. 'I'm only interested in what we can do for those who are still here. We know roughly how many there are in the valley and the ridge.' He raised his glass towards her, his voice now animated. 'You talk to all of them, Issy. I want to see if we can reach out further and coordinate something, to help our survival—'

Rus cut in. 'And reduce our isolation. We'll go backwards as a species if we stay disconnected. We can't stay stuck in survival mode, stuck at the base of the needs hierarchy. We have to start forming this new world into something we can leave to others… shape it to *their* comfort. Shape it into a kinder home.'

Issy sat down at the table, the three of them together again. Adam would join them later if he could, she'd explained. Rus hoped Adam would stay away. He hadn't told Charlie about Adam's offer to leave with him – it was a topic fraught with complexity. Charlie would surely misread it.

Charlie continued. 'I'm not saying we can do anything to change what's happened; we can't turn the world back to what it was.'

'Ah, now I understand,' Issy said, her tone musical, upwardly inflected. 'You're the last person I would've expected to take a romantic view of things, Charlie.'

'A romantic view? From me? Nah, you're confusing me with Rus.'

'I won't argue with that,' Rus said.

'Does *romantic* have a colour?' Issy asked him, suddenly diverted.

'Not for me it doesn't. Nothing more than the reds used in poetry or by Hallmark, but that's symbolism. It's different.'

'But *house* does?'

'As I've said before, yes. It's white. So is Saturday.'

'It fascinates me,' she said.

Charlie smiled broadly, flashing teeth as brilliant as the day. 'I had to do so much research when I first met Rus. Mythology, astronomy, synaesthesia.'

'Style, theatre, literature,' Rus added.

'Yep,' Charlie agreed. 'All those things were new to me.'

Issy clapped her hands, delighted. 'And you, Icarus, had to learn about farming and life in the tropics!'

'I'm still learning.'

'Do you have a colour for crows yet?' she asked.

'No, but that could change...' *Please don't ask about how colour associations can change*, Rus thought, suddenly regretting that he'd run with the topic, that he'd given such an insight into his thinking.

At that moment, Grant joined them, providing a timely distraction. He handed a sheaf of paper to Issy, and she started drawing a crude map – there was the valley, there the ridge, there Issy's little valley. Pointing to the valley proper, she said: 'I'm only in regular contact with you guys, the Farleys, the Aldises and Adam. I know the Hoppers are down there, but haven't had much to do with them. Up around the ridge, it's a little bit harder to see who's still here. The Parkers and the Dumonts are. And there are a few Kuku Yalanji families near the gorge.'

Charlie put his hand on the paper to stop it blowing away in the breeze. 'We don't all talk. But *you* talk to them, Issy, or know about them.'

'I like the idea,' she said simply. 'And I think you're right, Rus. We need to be more than isolated pockets of life. We need to be a community.' She turned to her husband. 'Tell them about your estimates, Grant.'

Grant scratched his beard sheepishly. 'I've been trying to estimate the number of survivors. I reckon there were around two and a half thousand people in this area a year and a half ago, most of them in the town. We can count just over twenty-five now, so that puts the survival rate at about one percent. In lightly populated areas, anyway, with around the same levels of crow infestations. In cities, I think survival would be close to zero. And it could be very different in other places.'

Charlie's eyes shone with interest. 'But it gives us something to work with.'

'And if it is consistent across boundaries,' Rus said, 'even though it sounds terribly low, that means there are still a lot of people out there.'

'And a lot of crows,' Charlie added.

Issy folded the paper. 'I'll make a bigger map, a more accurate one. And I'll start putting out feelers to those we know.'

She and Grant served them a light meal. Lots of vegetables and fruit from Issy's garden, and some barbequed kangaroo. As they ate, she looked to where the cars were parked, where the road wound down to the big valley. 'Seems like Adam's not coming. I know he's low on fuel for his plane.'

'I wanted to thank him for the crate of whisky.' Charlie sounded sincere.

Adam might yet break through to Charlie, but now Rus wasn't sure that was a good thing. Adam's compass, his changing colour, his tools – Rus wanted Charlie to be beyond those things.

Issy threw some scraps of food to the dogs. 'Rus, I'm assuming you haven't formed any theories from your flight?'

'Adam and I haven't had a chance to compare notes. We agreed we'd give it a few days' thought, then get back together and see if we could tease something out from what we saw.'

Charlie stood and ruffled Rus's hair. 'Another thing I've learnt from being with Rus. Perceive a problem, allow the subconscious to contemplate it – incubation is what he calls that – then wait for insight.'

'Illumination,' Rus corrected him. 'Insight is similar. It's the perception of things as they really are, but it's a subset of illumination.'

Charlie laughed, shrugging his shoulders, but there was pride in his eyes. And love. 'We should get going while the sun's still high.'

'Are you sure you want to stay here?' Rus asked Issy. 'You know I love this place, but it feels so vulnerable. You've got no barricades. The windows are exposed.'

'We'll be fine. We've only seen a few crows up here, and they never seem to stay. They stand outside our windows at night, and by morning they're gone.'

Rus stared at her, appalled. 'That sounds terrifying. I know you built this place with tempered glass, but still...' He shook his head, checking himself. 'It's your call, of course. And the offer remains open if you ever change your mind.'

As the truck pulled away from the house, Rus looked back at Issy and Grant, who stood there waving, their dogs tumbling around their feet, smiling, as if the world were still normal.

THE VALLEY XI

Charlie stared at the human scraps sprinkled near the chook pen. Rus stood beside him.

'Adam,' Charlie said, a simple confirmation that needed to be uttered. Rus let out a low, anguished sound, and the hens scattered.

They stood there for a long time. The branches of the tree swayed above them, the sun glittering through its leaves, entwining normal with abnormal, tranquillity with horror.

'I can't believe we didn't hear anything,' Charlie said quietly, needing to say *something*. 'The thunder must've covered…' He stalled, unable to complete the sentence.

'His screams?' Rus's words came out shallow and stretched, his lips barely opening to form them.

Charlie nodded. 'We couldn't have helped him, even if we'd heard.'

'He didn't deserve this,' Rus said. Charlie almost thought he was reassuring himself. A slight tremor moved across his frame.

'He didn't,' Charlie said. 'No one does.'

'He got so close to our house, Charlie. He almost made it.' Rus sucked in air, loudly, as if he'd just surfaced from diving deep underwater. 'My God, we probably drove right past him. He probably called to us, and we drove right on by…'

'We tried. We did, Rus. We really did try.'

Slowly, Rus straightened. Achieving his full height, he stood stiffly, almost in defiance of what was before him. Charlie imagined Daedalus. The mythology of Icarus was suddenly real, but twisted, subverted. It was Daedalus, not Icarus, who was dead.

'Our wings are gone,' Rus said, his voice monotone again.

Your wings, Charlie wanted to say.

Rus took deep breaths, his shoulders shuddering. Crying, uncontrolled and uncontrollable. Rus made no attempt to hide it, and Charlie made no attempt to soothe it. The crying was raw, it was needed. Charlie understood that.

When it had passed, Charlie felt a numbness descend upon him. He didn't want to admit it, but he was relieved that Adam was gone. It was the wrong thing to feel. Adam had been trying to form a connection recently, with his offer of the water of life, the crate of whisky. Charlie had wondered if things might eventually change between them. But now, he could own the truth more easily: he'd never trusted Adam. It was not simply a matter of like or dislike.

'We should bury him, or they'll finish their work tonight,' Charlie said. Then, an afterthought, but a reasonable one: 'Assuming it *is* Adam.'

'Who else could it be? Everyone around here is gone.'

'True.' Charlie folded his arms, not meaning to be defensive, but defensive nonetheless. 'We should have a ceremony of some kind.'

Rus nodded. 'Raise a toast to him.'

They stared at the desecration before them, not moving, for a long time. Then they gathered what they could. Torn pieces of skin, a half finger, a spleen, a kidney. Things they couldn't identify.

When it was time, Rus dug the grave and Charlie filled it in, after a few words and a clinking of glasses. The sun was high, birds and insects sang, but the world had changed again. And it continued to shrink.

THE VALLEY XII

The cane was still too wet to burn. They needed patience, but it seemed that Rus couldn't find any. He paced about the house with long strides, down into the yard and around the property, over and over. They still couldn't contact Issy. Rus wandered from room to room, as if he was looking for something, picking up photos, objects of meaning. Fiddich was gone, Adam was gone, Issy was silent, and Rus carried the weight of it all as if it might crush him.

After turning off the generator for the day and checking the defences and equipment, Charlie discovered that his flamethrower was gone. He found Rus quickly enough, not far from the western border of the cane fields. Rus stood in front of a crow. Its skin was grey and leathery, open wounds dripping yellow oil and drawing flies. Its belly was bloated, and its few tufts of remaining hair held leaves and twigs. Sharp thorns grew from its hands, some sprouting from its face. It was *old*. Rus was staring at it intently.

'Icarus,' Charlie said, as calmly as he could, 'what are you planning to do?'

Rus stood with the flamethrower's nozzle aimed at the scarecrow. Stalks of sugarcane rippled around them, moved by the slight breeze.

'They killed Adam.' Rus's voice was distant. 'They killed Farley.

They probably killed Fiddich.' His body shook as he spoke his list of the dead. Despite his height, he seemed small. 'They'll kill us next if we don't stop them.'

'We *will*, tomorrow. If you kill this crow now, you'll only get us killed too.'

'I want them to burn, Charlie. I want them to go, and I want them to feel pain.'

Charlie pointed over Rus's shoulder. 'There's another crow just there. You know they wake when one of them is under attack. And that's when they're fast.' He placed a hand on Rus's, angled the flamethrower down. 'I want you to be safe, Rus. I want you to be okay. Please be okay.'

Rus turned around slowly. His voice lost its edge, but it was still low and strained. 'I *do* love this place. You know that, right?'

'Yeah, I think I'm beginning to. But let's keep away from the flames for today, okay?'

Rus nodded, and they walked back to the house.

The sun set. The crows came to life, shuffling around the yard and under the house. Charlie and Rus watched through the shutters for a while. They counted eight. They tried to emulate a usual night, but faltered. And they tried at last to sleep, but there was no rain or wind or thunder to make the night sound normal. If sleep was the cousin of death – Charlie remembered his father describing it so – perhaps it was good that it stayed away tonight.

THE VALLEY XIII

The new day was bright, windy, and very hot. A good drying day for the tropics. A good day for a burn-off, hopefully. Rus felt sleep deprived, but a combination of coffee and adrenaline helped. He was focussed on the day ahead of him – not on yesterday, not on tomorrow – and that helped too; he *felt* again, but it didn't overwhelm him. And the shape that had been forming was contained, at least for now.

Rus tested some cane, but it was too green, too wet, to burn for long. 'Damn,' was all he said.

'We may have to wait for a few more days,' Charlie ventured, but he sounded uncertain. 'Or leave.'

'Leave? But you said—'

'Desperate times, as they say.'

Life is still here, Rus realised, *or it could be.* For Charlie, for him too. The roles of support had been reversed today. That had been the way of it over the years, and it couldn't be allowed to fail them now. 'Don't give up on the place yet. We might find a way. I'm clever with fire, remember?'

Charlie laughed, but it was brittle. The heaviness on Rus was descending upon Charlie too, and it was building. The lines around his dark eyes, etched by the sun and work, had grown suddenly deeper.

'If the crows aren't too close together, we might be able to take them out one at a time,' Rus said, more to himself.

Charlie nodded. It was a small sign of hope, and Rus ran with it. 'It would need both of us kitted up – one to do the burn, the other to defend if an attack happens.'

'But if there are a lot and they attack in numbers, we couldn't burn them in time. We'd die.'

'I don't want us to die, Charlton. We'll make sure we do it right. Let's go back to what we were doing two days ago: counting crows, finding out how many we're dealing with. Then we can decide if it's doable.' After a pause, he added, 'Maybe if we could get a better look, we wouldn't need to.' He turned abruptly and hurried from the field, up the stairs. Charlie followed.

Rus climbed through the trapdoor into the attic space. He made his way over exposed beams to a section of repaired roof, though *repaired* was perhaps not the right word. *Patched* was a better one. Rus punched at it, forcing open a small crack, and squeezed through it. He was struck by acrophobia when he attempted to stand up. The roof felt steeper than it had looked from the ground, and he was a long way from that ground. He got down onto his hands and knees and dragged himself carefully over to the edge of the roof.

'Not so graceful now,' Charlie called up to him, back in the yard.

'I really don't like heights,' Rus replied stiffly, but he was pleased that Charlie had lost some of the heaviness. 'I have to earn my keep, though...'

His words crumbled when he saw it. The fields were scattered with changed people, just visible among the cane. He counted at least twenty, heads down but angled towards the sun, as if following its movement. Rus's hands lost their grip in the heat and the fear. He slid towards the gutter, yelping, but his feet found purchase. He heard Charlie gasp.

When he was back on the ground, Charlie held him tight.

'There are so many of them,' he said. 'Too many out there. I think I was avoiding it – I didn't want to know. We should've done this sooner.'

Charlie frowned, then formed a lopsided half-smile, his dark eyes sad but focussed. 'We have to leave,' he said. 'Let them have this place. We'll find somewhere else.'

***

Rus lifted the photo of Charlie's parents. 'You should take this.'

Charlie took it, stared into it. 'I wish we had some of your pictures around.'

'I've still got my phone, and it probably still works. One day, I'll power it up, and then I'll have photos of my family again.'

'Whatever happened to them? God, I'm sorry we don't know. I'm sorry you were here when it all went to shit.'

When Rus finally responded, he sounded calmer than he'd expected. 'I wish I knew. It's killed me all this time, not knowing. How did my parents die, and Astrid and Nathan? My friends? When? Did they suffer? Did they become crows?'

'I know. I got to say goodbye to my parents... it's not fair.'

'When the phones died, that was the hardest. They were still alive then, all of them. I just wanted to call them one more time, to hear their voices one more time.' Rus was glad that Charlie had never suggested they might've survived. Glad he didn't suggest it now. It would've activated the white anger.

'Anger is sometimes caused by a sense of something not being right,' he'd once told Charlie, back when they lived in Sydney. 'It's caused by inequities, injustices, power imbalances. And it saves us from pain.'

Charlie had responded that anger, like drinking poison, hurt the ones who carried it. 'There's always pain,' he'd said.

Charlie had been right. And Rus felt pain now.

It's not fair. It wasn't, and the anger still lurked like a cloaked villain in the wings.

Charlie carefully packed the photo between some T-shirts. Rus hugged him once it was safely stowed away.

'I think we need to assume that Issy and Grant are gone too,' Rus said, pressing clothes into his backpack. 'We can't go to their place. And I was forming a theory. I thought I might've had *illumination* at last, but I've changed my mind.'

Charlie stopped packing. 'What'd you come up with?'

'It was partly from your analogy of saltwater crocodiles. When I saw the crows today, I realised how important the sun is to them – that's not new to us – but they'd all turned to follow it.'

'We know they like warmth, but maybe they *need* it,' Charlie said, following along. 'They don't ever seem to starve, though their food source is limited now.'

'And the city, with all of its concrete, holds the heat. A magnet for things that need it.'

'I think you're onto something, Rus. Why'd you change your mind?'

'Issy and Grant have never been surrounded. Crows come to their house but never stay. I wondered if that's because their place is covered by so many trees.' Rus paused at the thought of their friends being dead, at the thought of a theory formed from a flight with Adam. 'But if they're gone, then the darkness didn't deter the crows and my theory is flawed.'

'There may still be something to it. Issy and Grant might've left their property and opened themselves up to attack. Given time, we could test your theory.'

They continued to pack. Rus zipped up his backpack. 'Maybe we could go further up the coast, over the river. One percent of the population there would be small, but it would mean less crows too.'

'Or out to an island. There's plenty to choose from. I know Adam said he always saw lots of crows when he flew over the nearby ones, so we'd have to find one that's deserted. It'd be hard, but we could do it.'

'On an island, we'd lose any hope of forming a community or shaping things. We'd compromise what we are. I don't know if I want to live like that.'

'Me neither, but if it was just for a short time, we could, couldn't we?'

Rus nodded. He placed his bags at the back door and looked out at the farm. They were leaving. It was proving harder than he'd ever expected. He had seen so much horror, only yesterday he'd seen it, but this unravelling of home was a dreadful thing.

He knew it then, the colour for the word *home*. It was gold; it always had been. And this place glowed gold. Even surrounded by scarecrows, it glowed.

CHARLIE AND RUS I

They'd agreed to leave early the next morning, giving themselves the full day to find somewhere safe. One more night in Charlie's parents' house, now theirs. It almost seemed that Rus needed this time more than Charlie did. Again, Rus wandered around the house in the late afternoon, this time as if he was saying goodbye to it, pausing, delaying at certain points. Replaying memories, perhaps. Staying quiet.

Their bags were packed, mostly, and sat waiting at the back door, ready for their departure. Fiddich's food and water bowls were nearby, things that they didn't need to take. Fragments from yesterday hung in the air, fragments that needed to be spoken about, conversations half-started and in need of finishing. Charlie was relieved when Rus initiated that finishing.

Slowly, Rus stepped up to Charlie. He kept his eyes down. They roamed with mercurial movements, but became focussed, bright. He placed his hands on Charlie's shoulders. 'I'm really sorry, Charlie. For being cruel. I have been, lately. Over and over, I have been. I don't mean to be. You don't deserve it.'

Charlie smiled. Rus's words were sincere, and they were good to hear right now.

'I've always been like this. Cold anger's my thing, you know that, but it's not right. I'm sorry.' Rus let go of Charlie, and looked out at the sugarcane, through the back windows.

'It's okay. I know you never wanted to come here – I brought you here, and it was the wrong thing to do.'

'No, it wasn't the wrong thing. It probably saved us both, and I want to live. We've only got one go, right? I want to create meaning from it.'

The rubbing off goes both ways, Charlie thought. Of course it did.

'I've struggled, being here. I own that. I've been angry, not at you, not really, but angry at how things turned out. Angry at this way of life, I guess. Angrier when I remember that my family is gone.'

None of this was news to Charlie. He understood the anger, the mask it provided. For the last year, he'd known it was there, buried shallowly, and felt terrible guilt for it. He'd also known that Rus wasn't aiming for that effect.

'And you're angry that the world isn't fair, Rus. I get that. Angry that it changed a bit, but not enough. Not nearly enough.'

'Yeah, I am. I'm sorry you've felt that anger,' Rus said, as if reading Charlie's thoughts.

The sun reached into the kitchen. Rus's eyes dazzled in the warm light, but the lines on his forehead deepened. 'You're like Issy in a lot of ways, Charlie. You're never out of place.' His expression said *How do you do that?* but he added quickly: 'You never *seem* like you're out of place, at least.'

'In Sydney I was.'

'Nah, you didn't *want* to belong there – that's different. But you fitted in.'

'Belonging, fitting in, *blending* in… it's complex stuff, Icarus. And terribly painful for some. My dad felt that way, for different reasons to you, but I know what it can do to someone. I'm sorry the world is so fucked.'

'Not all of it is, not even now. My camouflage has never been so good. I wish I didn't feel the need for it, that's all.'

'In some ways, I hoped this farm would become a refuge for you, like it was for Dad.'

Rus's face softened. 'Strange that you say that… I'm starting to realise what this place means to me.'

The rubbing off was more advanced than Charlie had thought. 'Just as we're leaving it.'

'It's a bit of a *Big Yellow Taxi* moment. I wish it didn't need to be, but it is.' Rus beckoned Charlie to sit beside him in the kitchen. 'I've never needed that kind of moment to know how much you mean to me, Charlie. Please believe that.'

Charlie said it at last, didn't mean to, but it came out: 'I heard you and Adam making plans.'

'When?'

'Here, when he came for drinks with Issy and Grant. You were in the living room. I remember everything, even the record we had on.'

Rus became very quiet.

'It was Aldous Harding,' Charlie filled in for him.

When Rus spoke, it was in a subdued tone. '*Imagining My Man*… symbolic. Yeah, I remember it all too. There were no plans – nothing in them.' He pushed a hand through his hair. 'I always thought you heard us. I should've made this clear long ago.' His eyes flickered over the bench tops, over the window, flickered over everything and back to Charlie. 'We were drunk.'

'We all were. Does that change anything?'

'Not really.' Rus sighed. 'I think I was playing a game.'

'With Adam, or with me?'

'With myself. I was struggling, with this place, with the world changing. None of it was as I'd expected.'

'It's the same for all of us.'

'I know. But being here, even before everyone died – it wasn't what I'd envisaged for my life. I had to rethink everything. I hadn't got there yet, and then civilisation had to go and collapse on me.'

Charlie absorbed Rus's words. He'd had to readjust all of his expectations too, but in a different way.

'Those plans weren't real plans,' Rus said. 'I'd talk about flight, but I'd never have gone through with it. It was *fight,* not flight, that I'd always turn to. You know that.' He closed his eyes. 'It was a game to calm me, that's all.'

'Did Adam know that?'

'I think so. Probably. Maybe not… it doesn't matter anymore.'

'It does matter. To me it does.'

Rus's eyes shone with a watery-blue regret. 'I understand that, I do.' He paused for a long time. 'And because all of this matters, I need to tell you something else, Charlie.'

Charlie almost said he didn't want to hear it, exhausted by the idea of more secrets, more revelations.

'Adam asked me to go south with him, when we flew over Cairns.' Another pause, then Rus hurriedly added: 'I said no, and I meant it. Please believe me.'

It wasn't half as bad as Charlie had expected. His relief was powerful. 'I believe you, Rus. But you should've told me at the time.'

'Yeah, I should've, I know. I wasn't protecting Adam. I just didn't want to make things worse.'

Charlie considered Rus's reasoning. He almost questioned it further, but the events of the world and of relationships unfolded in their own way. Sometimes it was best to just accept this.

'I want to be here for you, Charlie,' Rus said. '*And* with you. I'm sorry for how long it's taken me to tell you all this.'

Charlie believed Rus. Believed him completely. The Rosetta Stone was found at last – that conversation, finally interpreted – those plans for escape, hurtful, but ultimately benign.

***

Rus had told Charlie the truth. It was a simple truth, and he wished he'd told it sooner. He knew it had eaten at Charlie. For a long time, he'd known it. *Why did I allow that?* Punishment, he decided, for things Charlie should never have been punished for. And pride, perhaps. The entwined shapes of anger and regret formed briefly then collapsed. Now was the time for letting go.

As they sat at the bench, Charlie smiled. Wanly, but with warmth. Rus wanted to make a special meal for their last night in this house. Briefly, he considered slaughtering a chicken and cooking it, but there had been enough slaughtering here. He couldn't bring himself to do more. So, it would have to be salad and fruit and eggs. And more of Adam's whisky.

The day ran itself down, moving at a protracted, reflective pace, but filled with sharp light. A day of significance, they agreed, but Rus suspected only he saw its vivid colours and wistful hues, its shadows and its outlines, the portents, and the meanings.

He fell asleep quickly that evening. Went deep under, could sense the going under as it happened, and was grateful to shut out the day. He woke to Charlie yelling.

'Get up – they're trying to break in!'

Sleep held Rus. Briefly, he thought it was a bad dream, but Charlie was moving in the dark, and he could hear banging, the sound of wood being punished by force. In the distance, guineafowl sounded their grating alarm call. Charlie held a flashlight and handed Rus one of the revolvers.

'How?' Rus managed to ask, and followed Charlie towards that terrible sound.

'I don't know. We raised the bridge.'

'Wanderers?'

'I *don't know.*'

They were not wanderers. As soon as Rus and Charlie arrived at the back of the house, they could hear the sighs and hisses of crows. The windows had been shuttered for the night and the brace across the door held, but the door moved with a rhythm that said it might yield to the attack. And there was a tapping sound. Across the windows and door, beneath the sound of the heavier blows, a constant tapping. Charlie and Rus dragged the old fridge from the kitchen and pushed it against the door.

'Check the front,' Charlie ordered, as he hammered loose boards across the back windows. 'But come back if there's any trouble.'

The rule of *never go alone* was broken by necessity. Survival depended now on independence.

Rus ran through the dark, tripped on something and landed heavily, but got back up in a fluid motion. He could hear shuffling from the veranda, all around, or so it sounded. The front door was silent when he got to it. He checked the brace, checked the locks. Everything was secure. He turned away, and it started. Fierce banging, and the tapping sound again. Rus dragged a bookcase from the hall, pulled it down so it collapsed almost on top of him, resting against the door.

Charlie arrived. 'We'll go to the attic, wait this out.'

'I want to see what they're doing first.'

Charlie tried to restrain him, but he slipped away with ease. Already, he was climbing, up onto the fallen bookcase, towards that terrible sound. He looked out through a small opening in the louvres above the door. The night was clear, full of stars that cast a pale blue light over everything, enough to make some sense of the world outside. A row of scarecrows stood along the veranda. They didn't seem to notice Rus. One hit the door again and again with a closed fist, while the others stood facing the shuttered windows. They tapped the wooden barriers with the backs of their thorny hands.

Charlie and Rus climbed into the attic and waited there, the assault on their home continuing, the tapping and the banging, rhythmic, relentless. The things outside wanted in. They kept up their wanting until the morning light seeped through cracks in the roof and magpies started to sing.

THE VALLEY XIV

The house had not been breached during the night. Charlie and Rus saw this when they climbed down from the attic. They removed the barriers from the back door and walked out into the cool morning. Chairs and tables were scattered across the back veranda, fragments of clothes, puddles of amber oil, all imbued with the fetid odour of crows.

Charlie pointed. The bridge was down. 'Fuck, one of the cables must've broken.'

'But they couldn't get in,' Rus said, as if it was a revelation, a marvellous one. 'Our house stayed safe.' He held the broken cable. It showed wear, which they'd missed in their daily checks. 'The crows were relentless last night. We've heard the stories, but we've never seen them like that.'

'We're lucky we didn't actually see much at all. But I know what you mean.' Charlie looked out at the field. The crows were completely hidden again.

'It looks so normal. So safe.'

'Saltwater crocs,' Charlie said simply.

They starting loading bags and supplies into the back of the truck. Food, water, weapons, books, whisky – plenty of that – and all the gas cylinders. Still no word from Issy or Grant, but there were other farms and stations on the ridge. They would find safety there. Keep moving if they had to.

Rus was quiet, but he seemed focussed and calm. 'I hope they survive,' he said, as he emptied some scraps for the hens and guineafowl. 'Especially the Charlie birds.'

'They'll be fine. They'll go feral,' Charlie replied. 'And in time, maybe we'll come back.'

'I want that, to come back. The crows will probably move on once we're gone, and we now know this place can withstand an attack.'

Rus's words came back to Charlie, amplified from the events of last night: *Too many out there.* 'We can't stay here while they surround us, waiting for us to make a mistake.'

'Don't overthink them, Charlton,' Rus said, with a smile. 'They're not intelligent animals.'

Charlie laughed. 'You're right. But don't underestimate the drive of a predator either.'

'It looked like the crows were trying to find structural weaknesses last night. And they knew what a door was, I swear they did. Perhaps they *are* more intelligent than we think.'

'I've been developing my own theory,' Charlie said, and Rus became attentive. 'We know the crows are changing, at a cellular level – their skin looks totally different. What if their code is being modified, and it's, I don't know... unlocking genetic memory, or something?'

'How would that influence their behaviour?'

Charlie shrugged. 'Maybe we're seeing an intrinsic yearning coming out as their DNA changes.'

'They want to be in familiar settings. Cities... and *homes*.'

'Just something to build into our theories. I could be wrong. It might just be food they're after, and they might still hold memories of what houses are for.'

Again, Rus smiled. 'Or it could be illumination, Charlie.'

'Regardless, you're right. The house is secure overall.' Charlie was glad that Rus wanted to return.

Rus walked to the base of the stairs and looked up at the house. 'We should repair the bridge before we go, so it's ready for us when we come back.'

Charlie studied the cables. It would take a few hours to dismantle the winch and rethread it all. 'It would need more than a quick fix,' he said. 'Though it would make it harder for crows and wanderers to get in, if we left with the bridge raised.'

'Let's do it,' Rus said. 'Let's make this place safe again.'

***

It took more than a few hours. When the bridge was finally working again, the sun was already throwing long shadows.

'Decision time,' Charlie said. 'Leave now, or wait till morning?'

Rus looked up at the house, over towards the west, where the sun hovered just above the ridge, then back to Charlie. 'One more night,' he said.

'You sure?'

'I'm sure. We can take turns keeping watch. But I don't think we'll have any trouble tonight.' Rus smiled in the golden light, his face abstracted by shadow and sun.

Charlie felt reassured by his calmness. Last night's attack was still clear in Charlie's mind. It was like the memory of a storm, of a terrible energy and danger that had been unleashed but had now receded. That storm, that energy, was intelligent, and it lingered not far away – he needed to remember that.

They resumed packing. Rus went back inside the house to collect more things. As he stacked items in the truck, Charlie heard the crunch of footsteps, from the wrong direction for it to be Rus. He turned and found Adam standing before him, his clothes tattered, his dark hair dishevelled, jawline covered in ragged stubble.

'My God,' Charlie said.

'Hey, Chuck.' Adam's voice was low and lacked its usual timbre. 'You goin' somewhere?'

'We're leaving,' Charlie answered, still processing this resurrection and all that it meant, especially what it would mean to Rus.

Adam looked out at the cane fields, then back to Charlie. He was gaunt, but his green eyes were as penetrating as ever. 'Good.'

Rus came back to the truck, said simply, 'Adam?'

Time seemed to stop. Adam was back, and all the dynamics that Charlie had put aside were in play once more. Strangely, Rus didn't approach Adam. There was a reticence in his posture, borne surely through seeing a friend he'd just buried walking once more among the living.

'We thought you were dead, that the crows had gotten you,' Rus said, very quietly. 'We buried you, said some words…'

'You've got a way with words, Rusty. I'm sure they were good—'

Rus cut Adam off. 'How are you here?'

'It's a bit of a story. Any chance I could eat first, and maybe get myself cleaned up?'

Adam's clothes were stained with dirt, and possibly blood.

Rus's face rippled with emotion. 'I'll get you some of my clothes, they might fit you… but I want to know what happened.'

'Is that doubt I hear in your voice, Icarus?' Adam said, perhaps jokingly, but Charlie thought he'd heard something in Rus's voice too.

'Not doubt, Adam. Everything's too surreal right now, that's all.' Rus stepped forward suddenly and hugged Adam, very tightly. 'But you're *alive.*'

'You know where the outdoor shower is, Adam,' Charlie said, taking back the conversation. 'I'll grab a towel and find you something to eat. Rus will get you some clothes.'

Adam moved towards the water tank.

'And then we can talk,' Charlie called after him.

Adam stopped briefly, but he didn't turn around. Soon, he was hidden behind the tank. Rus disappeared inside the house, and Charlie followed, turning back when he reached the veranda.

Below, hens scratched in the dirt. Only two days ago, the same birds had pecked at pieces from a human body; Adam's body, they'd assumed.

A rooster crowed in the distance. *We're reading this all wrong,* Charlie thought, and fought a sudden urge to raise the bridge.

***

The three of them sat at the table on the back veranda. Adam wore one of Rus's shirts. It stretched across his frame, but it fitted. He wore Rus's jeans too, but his feet remained bare. Charlie saw a distortion of Rus before him, familiar clothes on a tall human shell. It looked *wrong.*

Adam's hair was still wet. Now that it was combed, his green eyes gleaming, the old Adam seemed to resuscitate itself, bursting out of Rus's clothes.

'Thanks for the food.' Adam had eaten seconds and thirds, devoured each serving as if he couldn't get enough. 'I didn't have my hunting gear with me. I was about to improvise.'

'We saw your plane at the Aldises' place,' Rus said.

'Aldis lets me keep fuel there, or he did, whenever I could find some. Audrey convinced him to.' Adam finished his fourth serving, mostly vegetables and fruits. 'Any protein?' he asked.

Rus pointed out into the yard. 'Help yourself to one of the chickens. We've packed the best knives already; you're welcome to *improvise,* if you'd like.'

Perhaps it was humour, or perhaps it was damaged emotion, but there was another layer to Rus's words. Charlie focussed back on Adam. 'And?' he asked.

'I'd collected more fuel recently and stored it there. I was coming back for it and came across the bloodbath. Audrey deserved so much better.'

Charlie noticed it then. A patch of blood forming under Adam's shirt, on his left shoulder.

Charlie pushed himself up and away from the table, grabbing Rus and yanking him along. Adam stood almost as quickly. His hands came up reflexively, defensive.

'Is that from a crow bite?' Charlie asked, now full of accusation himself.

'Fuck, mate, I haven't been bitten. It's from a barbed-wire fence.'

They stood very still.

'What's with the twenty questions?' Adam asked. 'I came back to see that my mates were okay, and this is what I get?'

That seemed to soften Rus – a play on his emotions, an activation of affection, of loyalty. 'We looked for you.' He sounded almost desolate. But the hardness returned. 'You must've heard us. Why'd it take you so long to get here?'

'You want me to apologise for *surviving,* Rusty?'

'Of course not. I'm trying to make sense of this… it's not all stacking up.' Rus again spoke in layers, and Charlie felt himself deflected from the deeper meanings. 'You didn't shoot John Aldis, did you?' Rus asked quietly, almost apologetically.

'Now I see it, Rusty. You know I prefer the direct approach.' Adam held the moment, looked out at the cane fields. 'Aldis had just killed his kids. I heard the shots as I walked from my plane. He shot himself in front of me. Whatever his motives were, my arrival must've pushed him to act.'

'A murder-suicide,' Rus said, as if retesting the words, going back to Charlie and his original assumption.

'Yeah, that's exactly what it was. But I'd have killed him for murdering Audrey in any case. It would've been the right thing to do. You understand that, don't you? This isn't a game of soldiers we're playing, boys. It's real life, with high stakes.'

Adam sat down again. Charlie did too, and finally, Rus followed.

Adam let out a sigh. 'Hey, Chuck, you don't have any of that whisky I gave you, do you? It'd help bring the intensity of this inquisition down a notch.'

'We've packed what we can, but there's more.' Charlie looked at Rus, a signal for him to fetch it.

Rus returned with a bottle and three glasses.

'I'll pass,' Charlie said. Rus poured himself a small glass, handed Adam the bottle to pour his own.

'I didn't come via the roads, I crossed through farms,' Adam said, serving himself whisky with an expert hand. 'That's why I didn't hear you.'

'But it'd still only take half a day, max, to get from the Aldis farm to here,' Charlie said.

'It's a crazy world out there, Chuck. Things aren't quite as simple as they were. That includes walking between farms.'

'I'm really glad you're okay, Adam,' Rus said, after a long pause, his voice losing the brittle tones that had crept into it.

'We're just being careful,' Charlie added, relaxing a bit now that Rus had. 'It's about survival.'

Adam laughed at that. 'I know all about survival.' He poured himself another drink. 'And there are others out there who know about it too. I met a few of them on the way here. It's why I was delayed. You should be grateful I came across them before they came across you.'

Charlie considered Adam's words; they were disturbing on a number of levels. 'We're doing fine,' he said.

Adam stared at him with calm green eyes. They flashed briefly with an emotion that he couldn't read.

'Like I said, I just wanted to make sure you're okay, boys. And to say goodbye – I won't be coming back this way.'

A pause followed this revelation.

'It's almost like old times,' Rus said, his voice contemplative.

Adam's mouth formed a lopsided smile. 'Not quite, Rusty. Things have changed. But it's good to see you one last time.'

'Stay here for the night. We can drop you off at your plane tomorrow morning,' Rus said. He looked at Charlie suddenly, with apologetic eyes. His offer stung momentarily; it wasn't his to make alone.

Charlie forced himself to rise above his reaction. 'We've got plenty of bedding.'

'That'd be great. Not sure if I can sleep, but it would be nice to be comfy.' Adam poured three whiskies. He lifted his. 'To our final night together, boys. *Slainte Mhath.*'

THE VALLEY XV

Later that afternoon, Adam said he wanted to make himself useful. Rus had told him of their estimates – many crows, too many – and Adam wanted to see if he could hamper their movements around the house, maybe create some additional barricades. He put on a pair of Rus's runners that he'd found on the veranda and headed out. 'I'll be back in time for dinner,' he said, as if this were his home, as if it had been for a very long time.

Charlie had just finished splitting a log for tonight's fire. The axe blade had struggled to do its work; Rus would sharpen it tomorrow. For now, Rus carried an armful of wood towards the outdoor oven built by Charlie's dad half a lifetime ago. As he set the pieces down, a large beetle climbed out from one. It was dazzling in its reflective green armour.

'A stag beetle,' Charlie said, unprompted. 'A Mueller's stag beetle.'

'And I thought I was the only one who knew bizarre shit.'

Charlie's grin was wide. 'A wise person once told me our knowledge of such things is what separates us from other species,' he said.

Rus noticed the beetle's large mandibles. They gave the gaudy creature its practical name. He considered how they were used to attract a mate, or to fend off a rival. *Everything adapts,* he thought.

'Hey, buddy,' he said to the insect. 'Fly away home. Your house is on fire and your children are gone.'

'Pretty sure that nursery rhyme was about a ladybird,' Charlie said.

Rus shrugged. 'They're both beetles.' Almost to himself, he added, 'I wonder when... *if...* our house will be on fire. Or our fields, at least.'

The beetle climbed to the top of the wood pile. It opened its wing cases, briefly reflecting Rus and Charlie within them, then flew nosily away. It headed out across the northern cane fields, glinting gold and green in the sunlight. Rus followed it with his eyes for as long as he could. Even when it was gone, he kept staring at the fields.

Charlie asked: 'What's up?'

Rus turned back to the pieces of wood and continued to stack them. 'Nothing,' he lied.

Charlie shoved tinder into the oven. 'We're running out of the dry stuff,' he said. 'I'll put more under the house, in case it rains again.'

'I miss the weather apps,' Rus said. 'I can't make sense of the patterns up here.' That got a laugh from Charlie.

Rus realised he was staring back out at the fields. And Charlie was staring at him.

'We'll burn the fields off when we come back,' Charlie said. 'Promise.'

'That's not it.'

'Then what? Tell me, Rus.'

'Something just feels a bit off,' Rus said. 'Don't get me wrong,

I'm really happy it wasn't Adam that the chooks were pecking at yesterday.'

Another laugh came from Charlie. But he quickly became serious again. 'Yeah, I feel it too. The timing, or something... but all we've got to go on is what Adam tells us.'

'Yep, and so far, what he's said makes sense. Mostly. I've never known Adam to lie; truthfulness seems to be part of his code.'

'Maybe it's what Adam *isn't* telling us that we should be worried about,' Charlie said.

Rus wondered at this. 'Like you said, we can only go by his words.'

'And his actions.'

'And neither point towards anything significant.'

Charlie frowned, catching some look that Rus hadn't meant to give. 'There's something else. What is it?'

Rus sighed. 'I know it's silly, but since Cairns, Adam's colour has been changing.'

'I've never thought your colours were silly,' Charlie said, his expression gentling. 'I don't understand them, I admit that, but it's how your mind works.'

'I don't always understand them either. I think Adam is probably right – we're being paranoid, jumping at shadows. But I needed to hear him say he didn't kill John Aldis.'

'Would it have mattered if he did?'

'It'd depend on his reason, I guess. And hey, I'm sorry I invited him to stay, Charlie. I should've checked with you first.'

'We could hardly have kicked him out this late in the day.' Charlie laughed. 'Plus, I don't think anyone kicks out someone like *Adam*.'

'Having him here tonight may be useful, all things considered.'

Rus hoped Charlie wouldn't take that as an assessment of Charlie's capabilities.

Adam returned to the house as the sun's final few rays started to blaze on the horizon. He carried a guineafowl he had slaughtered, probably with his bare hands. 'For dinner,' he said, with a grin. He stared at the fire now burning in the outdoor oven. 'I'll cook.'

'You'll have to be quick,' Charlie said. 'The sun's sinking fast.'

Adam had already started plucking the bird, grey feathers fluttering around him in the breeze. 'We've got plenty of time.'

Rus watched the feathers. Some of them were sucked into the flames. He wished it had been a chicken Adam had caught, and not a Charlie bird.

***

The day ended with an incandescent sunset. Rus watched it from the front veranda, marvelled at its fractal beauty despite the terror of last night, the strange tension of today. The canvas of the sky morphed from pale yellow to deep bronze. Wisps of cloud lit up in oranges, then crimsons. Rus watched the world, its colours, his *naming* colours, change.

The crows arrived with the coming of night. Twelve of them stood below the repaired and raised bridge, heads down, silent, unmoving. Others shuffled around and under the house, tapping at the stilts, occasionally tilting their heads towards the humans above them.

The three men looked down at the crows from the veranda. Adam tossed bones left over from their meal down at the motionless figures.

'We try not to draw their attention to us,' Charlie said flatly.

'They know we're here, mate,' Adam said. He kept throwing

bones, and twigs when there were no more bones. 'I don't get it.' He turned very slowly to face Charlie. 'Why haven't you burned the crows from up here? I can do it for you. Easy.'

'They run when they're on fire,' Charlie replied. 'Not far, but if they go under the house, we could be in real trouble.'

Adam cast his eyes down to Charlie's waist, to where the handle of his gun was exposed.

'We'd waste ammunition firing at them,' Charlie said, clearly interpreting the look as a query. 'Their hearts, their circulatory systems, seem to be more integrated throughout their abdomens now. And that's the only way to kill them – it takes multiple shots, and we can't afford that.'

'Yeah, tough buggers,' Adam mused.

'Hence the burn-off,' Rus said. 'Still, we keep our guns close. Where's yours?'

Adam smiled wryly. 'I ran out of bullets, but guns aren't really my thing these days.'

In the distance, kookaburras farewelled the day. Something joined them, a bird that Rus didn't recognise. It sang a mournful song, lonely, tinged with beauty. Deep whistling joined the singing, more creatures that Rus couldn't place. Frogs, most likely. He wished they were closer or louder, so they could distract him from the sounds the crows made below.

'They're keeping an eye on us,' Adam said. 'Definitely getting smarter.'

Rus silently agreed. He wondered if Charlie might finally accept this observation too. Adam clicked his tongue as they headed back inside, back into the darkened living room.

'Rus and I plan to keep watch throughout the night,' Charlie said. 'Keep an eye on them keeping an eye on us.'

'I'll do it,' Adam replied. 'I don't think there's much chance of me sleeping, to be honest.'

'You should try. We've set up a comfortable space in the storeroom.'

'Nah, Rusty. I'm fine.' Very softly, Adam added: 'I have to keep guard...'

In the middle of lighting a third lamp, Charlie paused, likely wondering the same thing as Rus. *Keep guard against what?*

'It obviously wasn't me who the crows got the other night,' Adam said, at last. 'Someone else was here. A wanderer. That's what you call them, isn't it? There's more of them around these parts than you might think.' He went out to the veranda. 'They won't bother you tonight,' he called back.

Charlie motioned for Rus to go to bed. 'I'll take the first watch.'

'You sure?'

'I reckon Adam's going to crash any minute, no matter what he says.'

'I'll leave the door open,' Rus said quietly. 'Call me if there's anything strange.'

Charlie nodded. 'It'll be fine. I'll wake you in about four hours.'

As Rus walked down the darkened corridor to the bedroom, he heard the wire door open behind him. He turned. Adam had come back inside. He and Charlie stood there, two men made of the same stuff: dark shadows and flickering orange light, driven by pragmatism and contrasting codes.

'Good night,' Rus called to them both.

It had been a day of renewed hope. A friend had returned; it was possible that new connections might be forged overnight too. Charlie and Adam, friends at last, or at least not antagonists. Rus wanted that. Part of his want for the shaping of a new home.

***

When Rus woke, it was just after three. The night was quiet and still, but Charlie should've woken him by now. He headed to the living room.

A single lamp burned there. The others must've gone out, or been put out, and the diffused light was almost overwhelmed by shadows. Rus could make out Adam in that light, though, kneeling down, preoccupied.

Charlie lay on the floor. Adam loomed over him, a single hand gripping his throat. Even in the shadows, it appeared vicelike. Charlie's eyes had rolled back. Their whites shone in the orange light, and his hands grappled with Adam's, made an attempt at defence. The fight that Rus had come across was ending. Charlie's gun lay not far from him. But Rus's gun was now in his hand, pointed at Adam.

'What have you *done*, Adam?' he screamed.

The night erupted with a brilliant flash and painful thunder. The wall behind Adam burst into plaster shards. Rus had pulled the trigger without thought. Within that time of rolling slowness, Rus realised that Adam had cried out – the bullet had grazed him.

Adam fell backwards, his arms outstretched behind him, propping him up awkwardly. Then his right arm gave way. He rolled towards the back door, and sat there, very still.

Rus rushed to Charlie. Charlie was still *there*, his face terribly pale in the lamplight, but his eyes were open. Already he was trying to sit up.

Adam laughed. 'Well done, Rusty. I've been a good influence on you.'

Rus's rage was upon him, white and bright and blinding. 'You're fucking crazy, Adam.' He lifted the gun.

Adam matched Rus's white anger with his own red control. 'Don't be an idiot, Rusty. There are too many fuckwits left in this world. If you shoot me, there's one less good guy to help cull the bad ones.'

'If you think Charlie's one of the bad ones, you're truly fucked.' But Rus lowered the gun by an increment. Time had returned to normal, and he wasn't sure he could fire it so easily again. And Rus's anger was now tinged with red, tinged with Adam's old colour.

Adam held a hand to his injured shoulder. 'You've balanced things out,' he said. 'I like things when they're balanced.' He stood up, slowly. 'I never said Chuck was *bad*. He's in my way, that's all. And I told you I always remove impediments.'

Charlie had retrieved his gun and was standing now too, he and Rus side by side, protecting each other, protecting their home. Rus had no doubt that Charlie would fire if Adam kept provoking him.

Adam reached back. The door hadn't been secured, and he began to open it. 'This is the check-in I promised, Rusty... but your choice is pretty obvious.' He focussed on Charlie, his expression cold but lacking malice. 'And Chuck. No hard feelings. It was never personal.'

Rus waited, half-expecting another shot to ring out, but Charlie lowered his gun too. 'You tried to kill me. That's pretty personal,' Charlie said, in a raw and damaged voice, though it was surprisingly controlled.

Adam now had the door fully open. 'I was teaching you both valuable lessons, about chaos theory in action. It's what I do.'

'War crimes,' Charlie said, enigmatically. But Adam froze at the words. 'I remember reading about an ex-soldier. He did terrible things in Afghanistan but avoided conviction. That was you, wasn't it?'

Adam shook his head. 'I did what I needed to do. There's no crime in that.'

'Fuck off, Adam,' Charlie said, and motioned towards the open door with a flick of his head.

'You boys need to be a lot smarter if you're going to survive what's coming.' Adam backed into the night, stood briefly framed by it. 'You've got what it takes, Rusty. That's why I made you mine.'

The white anger returned to Rus. 'I was never *yours*.'

'Yeah, you were. So was Issy,' Adam said calmly, and vanished from view.

Rus and Charlie followed, but Adam was a shadow lost to the night. They heard him pound along the southern veranda, heard an earthy thud as he leapt to the ground. Starlight gave them a final glimpse of him before he disappeared down the driveway, to be hidden by sugarcane. Dark shapes followed him. The crows were fast when they hunted at night, and strangely silent. Soon they were gone too.

Rus and Charlie held each other. Speaking was suddenly impossible. Emotions came like a cyclone, turbulence swirling around them as they stood in the eye of the storm, momentarily calm. They shone a flashlight out to where the crows had been gathered. Half were still there, quiet, patient, watching without looking. Rus held his breath, expecting the night to be filled with distant screams, but they didn't come. Adam had escaped in darkness, and his name changed colour again, becoming blue-black like midnight itself, the colour of quiet transitions.

CHARLIE AND RUS II

It was mid-morning when they were ready to leave. The noise from the Cessna came to them, building up slowly.

'He survived,' Rus said, incredulously.

Despite everything, despite a throat that felt jagged and painful, and despite flickering images of the hands that had caused that pain, Charlie couldn't help but feel bitter respect for Adam. 'He does that,' he rasped.

Rus looked up briefly, then turned towards the house, but Charlie watched the small plane gain height and slice through the deep blue sky. He was hypnotised by this joint exodus, by the confirmation of Adam's survival and his leaving.

The plane disappeared. Soon, its noise was fading too. Charlie shuddered. He had survived an attack by the crows, but it was a human who'd almost killed him, one they'd invited into their home. Scars would form; he could feel them forming. But he and Rus had survived. Mythology continued to ripple and distort.

Rus came back to the truck when the farm carried only the sounds of birds and cicadas and wind. Charlie drew him close, feeling his breath, his heartbeat, his fear and his stillness. Rus was *with him*, as much as anyone could be, and even though that was a transient thing – *we are alone*, his existential tenet – it made life a much better thing.

The wind changed direction and brought the stench of death, worse than ever. It also brought the sound of a car, distant but getting closer. Charlie picked up the rifle, angled it to the ground, and Rus took his revolver from his pocket.

'Be ready,' Charlie said.

They moved behind their truck, where they could still see part of the long driveway. The vehicle was definitely approaching. Soon, it came around a corner, screened by sugarcane.

It was a ute. Issy and Grant's.

Charlie stepped out from behind the truck first, almost unable to make sense of this arrival. He looked at Rus, who stood there, gun in his hand, mouth open.

'We couldn't get onto you guys,' Issy said from the driver's seat, the window down, pulling the ute up next to them. 'Our radio died. We needed to check—'

'But we knew you'd be safe, you've got the best place for it,' Grant called over her.

'And we found something of yours.' Issy opened her door and Fiddich jumped out, followed by Issy's two dogs from the back tray. Fiddich ran back and forth between Rus and Charlie, turning to check if the other was still there, his whole body moving with his wagging tail.

'You're okay,' Rus whispered, as he wrapped his arms around the squirming dog. His face, bewildered and deeply moved, showed his failure to understand the world at this moment: it was not all terrible, and, once again, not as he'd expected.

Charlie spoke with sudden urgency. 'We should isolate Fiddich, in case he's been infected—'

'He's been with us for over ten minutes, Charlie,' Issy said lightly. 'Besides, you've both patted him. It's too late now.'

Pre-empting the next question, she continued: 'We found him running along the road not far from here. He was on his way home.'

'You came back,' Charlie said to the dog, the veil of last night's terror lifting suddenly and completely, at least for now.

'We saw the plane. Adam's alive?' Issy asked.

Charlie glanced at Rus, then nodded.

'Where's he going?' Grant asked.

'South,' was all Rus said.

Issy gave them each a hard stare. Her eyes lingered on the marks around Charlie's neck. Quietly, she said, 'Looks like we've got a lot to talk about. I really hope you're both okay.'

'You should've told us about his background, Issy,' Rus said flatly. 'More than you did.'

'I should've,' Issy replied. 'I thought I was doing the right thing.'

'Like you said, we've got a lot to talk about,' Charlie added.

Issy shook her head. 'I'm so sorry.' She blew out a long breath, reached into the cabin of the ute and pulled out a long, rolled-up piece of paper. 'I've finished the map,' she said, handing it to Charlie, as if to make amends. 'I really think it will help us.'

'But first,' Grant said, 'let's do something about your crow problem.' He and Issy pulled back a tarp on the ute tray. Under it were piled canisters of kerosene.

'For the burn-off,' Grant explained.

Charlie looked at the gift before them. 'We'll need all of this just to make it burn.' He struggled to get the words out through his own burning throat. 'It's very generous. Thank you.'

Issy came to stand next to him. 'It's no big deal, all things considered. And we need to stay human, stay connected – right, Icarus?'

Rus, with Fiddich by his side, nodded. 'We need to shape this place.'

Charlie and Rus helped unpack the ute. *Systems are correcting themselves*, Charlie thought, as he carried various incendiary items to their work area. *Human systems, at least.* He found meaning in that. Perhaps there was symbolism too. And now, the four of them would cause a return to the land – not quite as Charlie had thought it would happen, but fire could do it well enough.

***

They worked until dusk, carefully moving between and around the crows, laying tracts for fire. And when night came, so did the burning. The fields erupted with billowing flames and screams that echoed throughout the valley. Guineafowl and lapwings called out loudly, their screeches merging with the crows', a violent song that rolled across the farm. Charlie wanted them to stop, the scarecrows, the birds. He wanted all of the wrongness to stop and the quietness to return. Gusts of wind bore down on the burning cane, as if helicopters hovered overhead, spilling orange across the landscape. The screams faded, the birds became quiet again, but the fire continued to speak its flickering language.

They stood on the veranda, each sipping a whisky, watching the cleansing of the land in silence. The three dogs were alert, but quiet. Charlie turned, beholding his Icarus. The flames blazed in the copper of his hair, the blue of his eyes. He hadn't burned, wouldn't fall yet. Briefly, he was Arcturus again, a brilliant sun, and Charlie was blinded. He was glad of it.

'We can plant trees,' Charlie said. 'Test your theory. This is still our home.'

Rus smiled, aglow in the fiery night. 'It is,' he said.

www.ingramcontent.com/pod-product-compliance
Lightning Source LLC
Chambersburg PA
CBHW061218210726
48294CB00006B/1886